John McElgun

Annie Reilly or the Fortunes of an Irish girl in New York

John McElgun

Annie Reilly or the Fortunes of an Irish girl in New York

ISBN/EAN: 9783744708203

Printed in Europe, USA, Canada, Australia, Japan

Cover: Foto ©Andreas Hilbeck / pixelio.de

More available books at **www.hansebooks.com**

ANNIE REILLY

ANNIE REILLY;

OR,

THE FORTUNES OF AN IRISH GIRL IN NEW YORK.

A TALE FOUNDED ON FACT.

BY

JOHN McELGUN.

NEW YORK:

J. A. McGEE, PUBLISHER, 7 BARCLAY ST.

IN SINCERE FRIENDSHIP

TO

𝕭𝖊𝖗𝖓𝖆𝖗𝖉 𝕽𝖊𝖎𝖑𝖑𝖞, 𝕰𝖘𝖖.,

THIS VOLUME IS INSCRIBED

BY

THE AUTHOR.

CONTENTS.

Contents.

Contents.

Contents.

PREFACE.

ALL the sufferings under which the Irish tenant-farmers have labored, and still continue to labor, are not entirely owing to the bigotry and rapacity of their foreign and wealthy domestic landlords.

There is to-day another class of landowners in Ireland who are neither foreign nor wealthy, but who, by some means or other, have acquired sufficient to purchase a townland or two which have dropped off from some decayed estate, and who, in order to follow strictly the example of their exalted brothers, generally excel them in oppression and brutality.

So little has been said or written of this class in proportion to the magnitude of their evil-doings that I deemed it quite in place to draw John G. Ryan from their number.

Preface.

After all the poor emigrants have endured
in their native land, it is very distressing to
know the hardships and miseries that await
them, almost as soon as they lose sight of
the scene of the wrongs and cruelties into
which they have been born. Those especially who come to this country by way of
Liverpool, and have endured the importunity
of the man-catcher, and spent a night in his
loathsome den, and afterwards borne the
heartless insolence of the shipping-office,
must surely enter on the Atlantic voyage
burdened with far less hope than they carried across the Irish Sea. The description I
have endeavored to give of those English
institutions in this volume, so far from being
overdrawn, falls short of what I have actually witnessed myself.

Notwithstanding how often public opinion
has been directed to the coarse treatment of
steerage passengers by the ship officers, little or nothing has yet been done towards
abating the evil. The fault may not lie altogether with the ship-owners, but certainly

they are guilty of criminal carelessness in selecting such men as those to whose care they annually commit hundreds of thousands of lives. To observe the manner, actions, and conversation of some of these officials, a person could not help imagining that gross, vulgar, brutal ignorance was one of the qualifications on which they obtained their appointments.

Little better can be said of the worthy gentlemen at Castle Garden to whose tender care they are given on their arrival at New York. The latter dignitaries, however, have one very pleasant advantage over the equally mighty ship officers; that is, they are such fastidious, lively, funny, laughing fellows, and enjoy the sufferings, fears, and anxiety of the poor passengers so much, that it is quite delightful to behold them after the philosophic, stolid, British severity of the others.

A great difficulty with which the Irish girl in New York has to contend, is the fanatical bigotry of some of the mushroom employers

Preface.

of the city, masters and mistresses, whose bright minds are stored with such useful knowledge as they derive from the teachings of pious gentlemen like Rev. Dr. Brassman and others of that ilk. Now, let me remark that the mean, ungenerous spirit which prompts such people to take advantage of the dependent station of a Catholic girl, to insult and trample on her most sacred feelings, is as far from being American as cowardice is. It is found only amongst those low-bred creatures in whose existence not one spark of noble feeling can be found. However, sad to say, such wretches are not few, even in free America ; and, consequently, it devolves upon every intelligent Irish girl to study thoroughly the truths of her religion, that she may be able to repel the foul slanders against her creed, as Annie Reilly did.

THE AUTHOR.

ANNIE REILLY.

—•◦•—

CHAPTER I.

FARRELL REILLY'S HOME.

N the brow of a green sloping hill in
one of the most pleasant districts in
the beautiful province of Munster
once stood a small whitewashed cottage, shaded by tall poplars and neatly trimmed
whitethorns. In front of the cottage lay a
tastefully arranged garden, planted with choice
flowers, which, in the genial spring and warm
summer evenings, filled the little parlor with a
delightful fragrance. From the garden a charming view of the surrounding country could be
obtained: the high blue mountain in the far
distance, towering up till its top seemed lost in
the clouds; the dark and green forest stretching
out from the mountain base, till it fringed the
edge of the calm, majestic river which flowed
along it quiet grandeur to the Atlantic Ocean.
The inmates of the cottage, at the time our story

commences, were a man considerably advanced in years, his wife, and one son and daughter. Farrell Reilly, for such was the man's name, rented the small farm attached to the cottage from a neighboring magnate at an exorbitant rent ; but by honesty, perseverance, and skilful management, he never allowed himself to fall into arrears with his landlord, and, besides, contrived to maintain his family respectably. To his son and daughter he gave as good an education as the neighboring school could impart. Mrs. Reilly, who was a devout woman, of great good sense, carefully instructed her children in the true principles of religion, in order that they might, as she often said, " never wander from the true path when left to their own guidance." It is, and so well it should be, as we here know, the great object of every Catholic Irish mother who thinks there is a likelihood of her children coming to America, or going abroad into the world anywhere, to impress upon their minds a thorough knowledge of, and deep reverence for, the teachings of God and His Church. This religious training in the old land is the great reason why the Irish emigrant girl so far outshines in every virtue those who come to our shores from other countries.

When the worthy schoolmaster, Mr. Lacy, satisfied Farrell Reilly that his son and daughter

were as far advanced in the rudiments of education as his own ability permitted, the father told
them that, owing to his small means and total
absence of any prospect of bettering their worldly
condition at home, himself and their mother had
resolved on allowing them to seek their fortune
in America.

" For in that land, my children," said he, " by
faithfully practising the lessons your mother and
I have endeavored to teach you, you will find for
yourselves the means we are unable to supply you
with here. It is very, very hard, my dear children "—and poor Farrell covered his face with his
rough hands to hide the falling tears—" to part
from you, God knows, perhaps never to see you
again ; but our prayers will be heard for you as
well when you are far away as near."

Annie, then a handsome girl of sixteen, with
long, dark hair and pensive blue eyes, who had
been standing by the hearth, her hands clasped before her heart, went gently to her father's side,
and, putting her arms around his neck, said, while
she vainly tried to prevent her own tears :

" Father, oh ! do not let us see you cry ; it
breaks my heart to see you so distressed. Francis and I have long known we would have to
leave you and mother and seek a distant home
one day. You both have done all you could by

us, working hard to send us to school, and we
always pray to God that he may enable us to
repay you your great trouble with us."

"Yes, father," said Francis, coming to his
father's side also, " and sister and I, knowing
how much you toiled to do without our help
when we could have assisted you, will surely,
with God's help and your blessing, yet make a
happy home for us all."

" God grant it, my children !" said Farrell, clasping the hand of each ; "but how can I have the
least doubt?" And his face lighted up, and he
wiped the mist from his eyes. "You will not
fail. You are both good, wise children, and will,
I know, always continue so. Anyway," continued he, disengaging Francis's hand, and softly
drawing Annie to him, as he sat down on a low
chair, " it was rather soon for me to mention this
matter to you yet. I didn't intend doing so for
some time to come, but I felt strangely depressed
this evening, and you were both running through
my mind so much that I could hardly avoid act
ing as I have done. We cannot part for some
time yet. Mr Lacy tells me that you are both
as far advanced now as he can put you."

" Oh ! there is not a doubt of that, father,"
said Annie, looking around joyously on her brother who, with his face toward them, rested his

elbow on the old oak chest. " Francis and I could have told you that a week ago, but we preferred letting Mr. Lacy do it, as he promised us he would."

" I met him yesterday evening," said Farrell, " returning from his usual walk, and, after bidding him 'Good-evening,' I was about to pass on, when he placed his left hand on his side, and inserted the thumb of the right in the lower button-hole of his waistcoat—the ·sign by which you can tell he is prepared for a talk. I stopped on the spot, and, after a learned explanation of the causes that produce heat, and smoke, and wind, he told me there was no necessity for either of you entering upon another quarter, that both your educations were as complete—to use his own words—' as a full moon.' I thought I would never get home to tell your mother, and I don't think I ever went to bed happier than I did last night. In my joy, I did not think that what I had heard from Mr. Lacy would hasten our separation."

The smile on the father's face faded again, and it was evident to his children something unusual was annoying him. Francis said, after a pause :

" Father, nothing has happened to you since last night, when you were so happy? I wish you would be so to-night."

"Not a thing, then," said Farrell, rising and going to the window; "and still I would give a pound note to feel the same as I did last night As I said a minute ago, I should not have mentioned our parting to you so soon. You must both now assist me in every way, till we have enough to fit you out respectably. Till then, we'll say no more on the subject. Here is your mother coming back from the chapel. Not a word of this to her." And Farrell lit his pipe, and went into the garden for his evening smoke.

CHAPTER II.

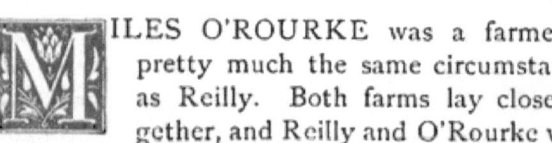ILES O'ROURKE was a farmer in
pretty much the same circumstances
as Reilly. Both farms lay close together, and Reilly and O'Rourke were
the best of neighbors, aiding each other in that
truly generous spirit which can be met with nowhere outside of Ireland. O'Rourke was a wi-
dower, his wife having died some years before,
leaving one child, James, then a bright, fair-
haired little fellow of six or seven summers.
James O'Rourke and Reilly's son, Francis, were
about the same age, and were playmates, very
much attached to each other. When at school,
they enjoyed their sport and studied their lessons
apart from the other children. Miles O'Rourke,
partly from the example set him by his neighbor,
was also desirous his son should have a good
education, and was very careful he should attend
every week as regularly as young Reilly. Annie,
who was about three years younger than her
brother, at length grew strong enough to be
carried to the school. At first, young O'Rourke

left the conducting of the little girl to and from school to her brother, contenting himself with carrying the two satchels and books, and occasionally lending Reilly a helping hand with his little sister over some narrow plank or brook by the way.

A year and more passed by in this manner, till at length Annie grew lively enough to skip along the way with her two companions, and join them in their plays. So much were they together, and so attached did they become, that the neighbors often remarked how much like one family they seemed. If Francis happened to be absent, and any of the other children offered any injury to "little Annie," as she was fondly called, James O'Rourke instantly became her champion and defender, and many a time he hotly asserted her rights in the division of fruits or lozenges, or her claim to be the winner of a game at "jacks." Annie, on the other hand, regarded him as a brother, and would seek his protection and advice almost the same as she would Francis.

Time went by, strengthening the affection between them, till at length they found they were lovers. This feeling came on each gradually, steadily, till it ripened into full bloom. The day, or week, or month it became such neither could tell ; and, as they looked back — if look back

they did—it seemed they had been so from in-
fancy. James had never told Annie of his love
more than by his manner towards her, and, yet
knew full well she was aware of it, and returned
it fully. Francis, too, soon discovered their regard
for each other. James would sing no song, as
they sat on the banks of the river or sailed along its
smooth surface in his father's fishing-boat, except
Annie first told him it was her choice. He would
gather no flowers for a nosegay in the garden or
on the hillside, except those that Annie loved;
and in the long summer evenings, when their
duties for the day were over, and he carried his
flute to the hill-top, Annie was compelled to call
for every tune he played.

Mr. Lacy, though not over-clearsighted in that
department of knowledge, at length saw that
James O'Rourke's and Annie's regard for each
other was something out of the common sphere,
as he termed it one day to a neighbor.

"You see," said the garrulous schoolmaster,
"it is very delightful to a man of my profession,
whose first duty it is to study the minds of my
young charge, and watch the gradual expansion
of the intellect, to be able to do so thoroughly.
I have seen boys acquire a regard for each other
when at school that they afterwards carried into
the world, till one would actually lay down his

life for the other.   When I see this feeling in **two**
youths, I make it a point to always encourage
that feeling, providing it does not extend to
prompting in the class.   Then," continued he,
with emphasis, " I leave nothing undone, at whatever cost or pain, to eradicate that evil.   I have
always," and he nodded his head sagely, " given
myself, in common with other learned and wise
men, credit for my great knowledge of human
nature.   The slightest iota gives me a clue.   I
can tell by the manner in which a boy or girl
keeps his or her hands clean, and his or her hair
combed, to what degree he or she may rise or fall
on the platform of life.   My experience is so
long and so varied," continued he, rubbing his
ear, " that I did not believe there was a crevice
in the heart of any boy or girl I could not ex-
plore ; but I find "—this in an injured way—" that I
have been deceived ; yes, deceived badly, and by
a youthful pair who have grown up under my
very rod and eye.   I allude to the daughter of
Farrell Reilly and the son of Miles O'Rourke.
That they should be friendly to each other, their
parents being such agreeable neighbors, is in no-
wise strange—friendly, I mean, in the ordinary
way.   But 'tis puzzling," and again he rubbed
his ear ; " the friendship of those children for each
other goes beyond my comprehension.   Both are

very lively at their tasks, and I often watch them assisting each other in their preparation; but in class, though they stand side by side, one will never be found prompting the other. I always find both understand the lessons exactly alike, and, if one happens to be absent, the other will be like a bull in a mist for that day; and I have grown so accustomed to this thing now, that I cannot find it in my heart to punish the delinquent, because I know the cause so well. Little Annie's brother, I find—and that deepens the mystery—though just as clever as either, understands his lessons altogether differently from them. The most ordinary person," he went on, with a sweep of his arm, "would expect the similarity to exist between the brother and sister, and not between two who have not a drop of each other's blood in their veins; but the thing is just as I say. I have given the matter a good deal of consideration, and the only point I can arrive at is that, when those young people grow up, if they do not become one, I was born and will die an unqualified lunatic."

CHAPTER III.

HEN Mrs. Reilly entered the cottage on her return from the chapel, on the evening her husband and children held the conversation related in the last chapter, Annie, who ran to help her mother remove her shawl, noticed how pale and agitated she was. Annie, greatly alarmed after the signs of trouble in her father a few minutes before, asked, while her hands trembled with apprehension, and a flood of tears came into her eyes :

" Mother, for heaven's sake, what is the matter with you?"

Mrs. Reilly hesitated for a moment, her lips quivered, and her look became more ghastly; then she pressed her hand to her forehead, and said :

" Nothing, I hope, child; tell your father to come here quickly. I want to speak to him a moment. I have something to tell him. I should not, if I could have prevented it," she added to herself, sitting down in the chair from which her husband had risen, " have exposed my distress to you, and anyway the alarm may be groundless."

Annie's frightened look and manner, when she ran to him, so alarmed Farrell that he dropped his pipe on the garden-wall, and rushed breathlessly into the house. Mrs. Reilly rose to her feet, and tottered against the wall as she did so.

" Farrell," said she, " we can rely on Annie's good sense to keep what I am going to tell you from Francis. Thank God! the poor boy is not here now."

" Oh! certainly, mother," said Annie, kissing her fervently; "you know I would tell Francis nothing that would annoy him."

" Tell us quick, whatever it is," said her husband, throwing his hat on the floor. " It is something dreadful, I know, for my heart is breaking all day."

" Well, it is this, Farrell," said his wife: " When I was leaving the chapel-gate this evening to come home, I saw John Griffin Ryan, as he calls himself, just going past, in company with a tall, big-whiskered, ill-favored-looking man. I was drawing the hood of the cloak over my face, for it looked like rain, and turned my head away; for I never like speaking to Ryan, he is such a false-hearted hypocrite, and carries such an ugly, deceit ful leer on his face. The corner of his eye caught me, and he said something quickly to the other man, and both turned round and met me in the middle of the road.

"'A good-evening to you, Mrs. Reilly,' said Ryan, stopping my way.

"I returned his salutation without raising my head, and moved to get past him.

"'Mrs. Reilly,' said he, moving before me again, and, as I looked up, a broad grin covered his big, pasty face, 'this is Mr. Crofton, our new distinguished neighbor. He is thinking of settling permanently amongst us, and wishes me to make him known to some of our best people around, and you are just the first we met since he made the request; and, in truth, a splendid beginning, Mr. Crofton.'

"'I wish the gentleman well,' said I, again trying to get past.

"'Mr. Crofton is an English gentleman, Mrs. Reilly, and is a great acquisition to this community,' said Ryan. 'We must all try and learn something from him.'

"Though coming from the house of God, I could not keep down my anger, and I said:

"'We are not so very backward in everything here that any man, even though he is from England, can be set up as a model for us to imitate.

We are always anxious to learn anything profitable, but not to utterly disregard the old knowledge, as you have seen fit to do, Mr. Ryan.'

" His face reddened like an oven, and he tried
to give one of those vulgar, loud laughs of his,
but was not able.

" ' Oh! you are on your *sharps* to-day, Mrs.
Reilly,' said he; ' but I can well afford to let you
go on. Can't I, Mr. Crofton?'

" The other made no reply, but gazed at me in
a half-stupid, idiotic manner, with his eyes almost
closed, and his mouth open.

" ' I always make it a rule to be nice and civil,
even when doing something very unpleasant to
me,' said Ryan. ' I always practise that, Mr.
Crofton, and I find it never fails. I introduced
you to a gentleman this evening, Mrs. Reilly, but
that is not all my business. Tell your husband
to meet me at my office to-morrow morning at
nine o'clock.'

" ' If you have any business—and really, I don't
know how you can—with my husband,' said I,
' it is just as fitting for you to call on him.'

" The same ugly smile came on his face, and I
dashed away from them.

" I felt so annoyed, after this strange interview,
that I was hurrying along as fast as I could, when
who did I see coming towards me, running along

like a madman, but Miles O'Rourke. When he
saw me, he hastened even quicker; and, as he
approached, I could see he was wringing his hands,
and that the heavy perspiration was falling from
his brow.

" 'What is the matter, Miles?' said I, when
he came near enough to hear my voice. " Nothing wrong with you, I hope?'

" 'Wrong with me? O God in heaven! we
are all ruined, beggared, driven to the poor-house,'
said he, panting for breath; 'look at this—read
it.' And he pulled a paper from his breast-pocket,
and pushed it into my hand.

" Hardly knowing what I did, I glanced over
the paper. It was a notice to quit, signed by
Crofton and Ryan. A thick mist overspread my
eyes, my limbs grew weak, and I would have
fallen, only the heart-broken man caught me.

" 'What can be the meaning of this, Miles?'
said I, when I recovered strength to speak.
' Why is Ryan's name to this? He has nothing
to do with this townland.'

" 'O heaven help us! He has,' said Miles.
' I heard a rumor a few days ago, but gave it no
attention, that Crofton and he were seen together about here, and that Saunderson was
about to sell them this townland. I thought
'twas only idle talk; but, to our grief, the thing

is done now. I am going to Ryan to ask an explanation; and, if he is determined to ruin us, he will drive me to do something desperate.'

"I begged of him to come back, and consult with you; but he answered, 'No use, Mrs. Reilly; what can we do for each other now?' and walked swiftly on towards the town."

Farrell, who, during this story, had been pacing up and down the floor, his hands clasped behind his back, stopped suddenly, and, turning to his wife and daughter, said, "What Miles told you is true. We are ruined. That low, mean, sneaking turncoat, that he may win favor with this Englishman and with the other bigots around, will not leave one Catholic family on the land. You know 'tis the only way he has got to obtain even a nod from them; for, bad as they are themselves, they despise him, because they know the contemptible, crawling hound he is."

"O heavens! no, Farrell,' said Mrs. Reilly, "it cannot be; it will never come to that with us, that he will drive us from our old home. God is good and merciful; nothing so bad as that can happen. It is a way he has taken to let us know we are in his power."

'Ah! no," said Farrell; "I wonder at you, who know Ryan so well, to talk in that way. Is there anything too bad or too mean for him to attempt?

—a man who allowed his own father to black the
parson's boots, and, when he grew too old for that,
permitted him to be taken to the work-house,
where he was starved to death and buried in a
pauper's grave. Yes, buried in a pauper's grave :
and Ryan himself that day spent hundreds of
pounds purchasing pork for the Liverpool market."

"Oh ! may the Virgin Mary protect us from
the power of such a man !" said Annie, falling on
her knees beside her mother, who had knelt down
to beseech Heaven to avert the dreadful impend-
ing catastrophe.

Farrell said nothing to interrupt their prayers,
but stood, with God knows what anguish of heart,
looking out on the beautiful valley below, on
which the rich dew was falling plentifully. The
corn-crake's loud call from the meadows of tall
grass, the sweet notes of the nightingale, the
deep bark of the faithful watch-dog, all the plea-
sures of the summer evening which he, till that
night, enjoyed so much, only added to his load of
sorrow now, by reminding him they were scenes he
could not much longer enjoy. The tall white and
red rose-trees, now in full bloom, peeped sweetly
over the garden wall, or in at the little parlor
window, as if to softly whisper words of consolation and peace. Farrell leaned against the door-

post for some minutes, then raised his eyes, and, glancing around on the beautiful scene, smote his forehead, and re-entered the cottage. Mrs. Reilly and Annie had just risen from their knees, and began to offer all the consolation in their power to the distressed man.

" Now, Farrell," said Mrs. Reilly, " we are not certain yet that any such step as we dread has been taken against us. Remember, we have not been notified as Miles has. In the name of God, do you prepare in the morning, and go and see Ryan. What he wants to see you about may be to make some satisfactory arrangement with you. If he intended putting us out, he would not, I am sure, send for you. We will place all our hope in God, and not give ourselves up to grief and despair; 'tis time enough to deal with misery when it comes, and not invite it."

Farrell shook his head, and, resting his chin on his hands, sat silently till Francis came back from leaving the cattle at their accustomed resting-place, when, after a fervent evening prayer, they retired for the night.

CHAPTER IV.

SHOWS SOME OF THE QUALITIES OF THIS VERY HONEST MAN.

OHN GRIFFIN RYAN, " Pig-Jobber and Hog-Slaughterer," as the wide, dirty sign over his shop-door, in one of the back streets of the town, proclaimed to all who run and read, combined so many qualities in one body that our readers must learn a little more about him than they may be able to glean from the remarks of Farrell Reilly and Miles O'Rourke. As to the extremities of his name, very little need be said, " John " and "Ryan" being very common and very familiar names ; and there is no reason why they should not look very well, and get along very agreeably when put together. Many a less important man than our subject thrives very well with a far worse name. But why this extraordinary man chose to put those nicely-fitting names apart by inserting another between them requires some little investigation. That John G. Ryan was a thorough man of the world, his worst enemies never dare deny. John boasted of the quality at least

twenty-five times every day, and no man had the
hardihood to contradict him. John never said he
was simply a man of the world—oh! no. He was
a literary man besides; but he never chose to cultivate that quality. He possessed it; the mine was
there, he knew, but he kept it secure from the vulgar
gaze, without parade, further than to strike himself
on the breast, and say, "The blood of Gerald Griffin
flows there"; but more calm and majestic than
in the veins of the great poet himself. Yes, Ryan
claimed to be a relative of Gerald Griffin's. How
or in what manner, when pressed for an explanation, he knew not. He lived at a safe distance
from those who knew the poet's family, and,
shrewd man as he was, always took care to avoid
the subject when business led him to that part of
the province.

Well, being a blood relation of Griffin's, John
Ryan condescended to acknowledge the former
so far as to give room for his name between his
own—took him to his very heart, as it were, and
signed himself in very fat letters, when he learned how, "John Griffin Ryan."

Ryan was a great philosopher. No man, living
or dead, knew better than he how people should
conduct themselves in adversity. He could lean
back in his greasy arm-chair, his fat face showing
every sign of entire satisfaction, and lecture a

poor cripple, or paralyzed beggar, for fully two hours, on how they should bear up against their trials; and in the end, as if to see the fruit his advice bore, dismiss them without a half-penny. Ryan was a very great knave.

We have it on no mean authority that his reason for changing his creed was, that he might obtain the contracts for supplying pork to the military barrack. This little trick he could not conceal from his neighbors; but whenever he went abroad to any of the neighboring fairs, he always carried a pair of beads in his pockets, and always took care to display them as if by mistake, when making a bargain.

If the town or village happened to contain a chapel, Ryan was sure to be seen at Mass on the fair morning, and always walked from the chapel into the street bare-headed, while his flat gray eye glanced nervously up and down, lest some member of his new creed should see him. This happened once; but Ryan's ready wit quickly relieved him of all suspicion.

The minister, whose church Ryan attended when in his native town, happened to be driving past and saw him, hat in hand, leaving the chapel. The minister pulled up his horse instantly, while a tide of holy horror mounted up his throat from his very heart, which was a considerable dis-

tance. Ryan s horror was not much less, though
of a different kind. He bowed low to the minister—so low that the crown of the hat which he
held in his hand came in contact with the road,
and received a very ugly dinge. But Ryan heeded
this not. He sprang to the side of his worthy
adviser's car, drew his cuff excitedly across his
brow, and said:

"O Mr. Scollop! your reverence, I have been
horrified to-day. The thing is going too far;
they are actually planning the foundation of a
new popish chapel here. I heard so when I came
here to-day, but could not believe it till I have
satisfied myself by going in there just now. It
makes my blood boil, Mr. Scollop." And he shook
the hat downwards, as if it contained some of the
hot liquid, and drew his cuff again across his face.

The tide of holy horror at this information was
beating around the worthy parson's ears; but
Ryan's fervor caused it to ebb, and, after a firm
grip of the hand, he drove away. Ryan turned
away, too, and joined a crowd of farmers who
were looking on at the scene, and probably told
them he was threatening to assault the parson.

Ryan was gifted with an Indian Ocean-ful of
family pride. Although just as convenient to
him as Parson Scollop's church, his dignity would
never allow him to go to the church of the parson

whose boots his venerable father was said to black-
en. Now, we hold there is nothing at all discred-
itable in blacking boots. Many of our own boot-
blacks here have grown up to be wealthy and
respectable citizens, and would never blush to
confess they earned an honest penny with the
brush. Ryan being a philosopher, as we trust we
have established, it is hard to say how he would
have felt had his father followed the blacking art
in his rising years. He would, we venture to
hope, have borne it with stoical fortitude. But in
his early days, the man to whom the world is
indebted for Ryan sported the gorgeous livery of
a country gentleman's coachman : or, as the case
most likely happened to be, a country gentleman's carman. Nothing is more certain than
that he occupied one or the other of those daz-
zling positions ; for numerous old men and women,
who distinctly remembered that day, could tes-
tify they saw him with the lace hat on, but would
not commit themselves by declaring they saw the
lace coat ; so that whether he wore the latter
distinguishing garment or not must be left to
conjecture. The old gentleman had fallen in the
world—a thing his son could not tolerate in any
man, much less in his own father ; but he called
the family pride to his aid, and knew him no
more

Ryan was a very great hypocrite. We do not use the term in an offensive sense, but merely as one of his manifold traits. There are many hypocrites to be met with in every part of the world so closely resembling one another that a description of one would serve for all. But Ryan possessed all his qualities in an eminent degree; each shone out brilliantly. Ryan could commit the most base and grievous wrong on any of his fellow-men, and at the same time shed tears in the fulness of his heart over that man's sufferings; and declare, while his voice grew husky with emotion, and his arms swept the air in a paroxysm of Christian charity, that he could lay down his life for that man. Any one who had not the pleasure of an intimate acquaintance with him, and saw him while he planned the ruin of a neighbor, could not help thinking, or, if he were excitable, exclaiming: "Behold him! there is a true friend to all mankind."

Ryan was a liar, a great liar, a skilful, cunning, systematic liar. When a stranger entered his employment, and Ryan saw a likelihood of his proving useful, he would, before the second day passed by, promise the fortunate adventurer a share in the business; but always prefaced this offer by giving it as his advice that he had better, in the meantime, work for little or

nothing; and, as few could be found to withstand this luring temptation, many did take
Ryan's advice. Time would pass on, and
the day for taking in the new partner, who
probably by this time would have reached an advanced stage of starvation, would come. At no
period of his life would Ryan look so innocent, so
childlike, and so oblivious of earthly things as on
that day. His thoughts were no longer of earth ;
they had penetrated the clouds, and clustered
around the throne of the Deity. Ryan—bless
him !—would take off his hat and coat, and, sitting
down in his chair, let his head fall sadly on his
hand, dilate in soft, low murmurs on the short-
ness of life here below, on the length of eternity,
and how little we should care for this world's
"vile dross." When the hungry expectant, who
probably rose by daybreak, hardly condescending
to notice such of his acquaintances as might be
abroad at that hour, so much did his dignity rise
at the prospect of being John G. Ryan's partner,
would, seeing John so absorbed in heavenly
things, venture to remind him of his promise,
Ryan would gently tell him to leave him to his
meditation that day. Of course, the following
day the subject would be again brought under
Ryan's notice. His astonishment was unbounded.
He never heard of such a thing ; did he employ ?

madman? When or where did he make such a promise? Where was the witness? His indignation rose, till he ejected the deceived wretch from the place, with the comforting advice to secure his bondsmen, as he, John, intended having him arrested for robbery, or larceny, or some other disgraceful offence. Some minor intellects say it is only needful to tell the truth when a lie will not suit. But Ryan was no compromiser. He never saw the necessity of telling the truth in any of his transactions, and he throve on that determination. Well, there is a prince in every trade. We will not call Ryan a swindler. No. The example he made of an intended partner, who modestly ventured to add that quality to the chain, deters us.

Ryan was sitting in his office, elaborately commenting on the bright world opened up before a young man who stood before him, and whom he had entrapped the day previous, when Farrell Reilly and Miles O'Rourke entered the establishment. He had merely time to dismiss the young man with "God bless you!" when the two men came into the office. Ryan rose and extended his hand to Reilly, while he said, with the accustomed leer, "Farrell, I am delighted to see you there is nothing one man could do for another I would not do for you. Take a seat, sir."

Miles stood by the office door, but Ryan seemed not to notice him. Farrell sat down on a low form which extended along one side of the office, and Ryan wheeled his greasy chair around to get a better view of his face. " I don't really know how I feel this morning ; I see you look splendid. My men here are so much attached to me that it overpowers me. There is a young man just gone out there, and he is after telling me he'd rather work for me night and day than get into the Bank of Ireland. Did Phil say that, Ned ? " continued he, addressing a long, lean, crooked-eyed, ill-clad youth, who, planted on one knee, was scratching with a quill pen in a greasy book which lay on a low, flat bench before him.

" Yes, sir; and more, sir," said the well-trained youth, turning his face towards his master and Farrell, but with his eyes on the opposite wall.

" Ah! I am so forgetful. What else did he say, Ned ? Keep down your head while you're talking."

Ned almost struck his nose against the desk ; but, being an inquisitive youth, one of his eyes rested on Miles's face, where it remained, to the great horror of the latter.

" Phil said, sir," he went on, " that he never knew what comfort or happiness was till he met with you, and that his mother thinks he must be in heaven."

" Ah! poor woman," said Ryan, rolling his eyes along the ceiling, " she is a widow. I never wronged a widow. Evil tongues may say I have. I would wrong myself, I would wrong myself to help a widow. That is my nature, Farrell. I can't help it ; neither do I want to. I am a public nuisance—I mean a public institution, Farrell. Some are grateful, some are not ; but whether they are or not does not interfere with my claim beyond the skies. When an injury is done to me, I am always ready to forgive it ; that's me, John Griffin Ryan."

" You sent for me, Mr. Cary," said Farrell, who had not spoken since he sat down ; " may I ask what for ?"

" Yes, yes; so I did," said Ryan, stroking his chin. " I chanced to meet Mrs. Reilly. Farrell, you ought to be proud of that woman, so handsome, and so clever in her remarks besides. I met her yesterday evening when *me* and Mr. Crofton were going up the street. I introduced Mr. Crofton to her, and I don't think she cared much for the compliment. She is very *independent*, I tell you. My opinion is this," and his gray eye glistened villanously : " it is all very well for some people to be independent. I only say that **as**

my opinion ; other people may think differently."

"Well, Mr. Ryan," said Farrell, rising, while he
bit his lip to restrain his anger, "is this all you
want with me ?"

"No, sir," said Ryan in a loud voice, "'tis not :
but, if your time is so precious that you cannot
wait till I am done, you may go."

"I came here to listen to all you had to say,"
said Farrell, his heart sinking.

"Do you know, sir," said Ryan, "that I am
your landlord ?"

"I have heard so," said Farrell, "but was not
certain of it till now."

"You may be certain of it," said Ryan pomp-
ously. "Ned, when did we get the deed of that
townland, *me* and Mr. Crofton ?"

"Day afore yesterday, sir," replied the youth.

"Yes, so it was the day before yesterday," said
Ryan, nodding his head. "You see, I have so
much business to attend to, Farrell, that I cannot
remember dates at all. I want to tell you now,
Farrell—you know the great wish I always had
for you—quietly and in a Christian way that I
have let the whole townland to one man. It is
the most profitable way for me, and will give me
the least trouble."

"O great God ! Mr. Ryan," exclaimed Farrell,

smiting his forehead, and sinking back on the seat, " you would not do that. You would not send adrift an old family whose ancestors have lived on the land for a hundred years."

" Mr.Ryan," said Miles, in a hoarse voice, bursting forward, and speaking for the first time, " surely you are not in earnest. We will pay you any rent you choose, if ourselves and our families starve."

Ryan's gray eye turned on the last speaker, and he said slowly and emphatically : " You are in the hands of the law, sir ; go out from this place. I will give some of your family an opportunity to starve. The diet on Spike Island is very low, and the air very appetizing. You can tell your son that." Then, turning to Farrell, he went on : " You say, Farrell, your ancestors have lived on this townland of mine for nearly a hundred years ?"

" I can prove it, sir," said Farrell. " My grandfather was born in the house I live in now."

" Don't you know, Farrell," said Ryan, in a persuasive manner, " that this is an age of improvements ? All the old institutions are giving place to new ones. Mighty changes," continued Ryan, remembering a line he had read that morning in an old newspaper, " are going on around us every day, and we find no man grumbling. I did not

think, Farrell, that you, of all men living, would
set yourself against the tide. I thought I had
only to mention the thing to you, and you would
be delighted to find this revolution coming home
to us. Your wife, I know, wishes things to remain
as they are; but I did not think she could influence
a man of your sound understanding.":

"Oh! 'tis nothing new, as you know very well,"
said Farrell, "for foreigners to drive us from our
homes. *That* is one of the oldest institutions
of this country; and surely you, a man brought
up in our midst, would not follow their example."

"Let me go a little further," said Ryan, with
dignity. "Other landlords have taken their hold-
ings from people, and, rather than let them live
on the land, preferred to let it lie waste. Now,
what I am going to do is this: I will rent the *hull*
townland to one good Englishman, who will in-
troduce everything English and grand into the
parish, and make us thoroughly civilized; for we
are in a backward state, Farrell."

"How can you talk so?" said the latter, for-
getting his danger in the height of his disgust.
"Are you not an Irishman yourself?"

"I don't know, I don't know," said Ryan, standing up and straightening himself to his full
height. "I am not sure about that. My fore-

fathers were Normans—the Carews. I may have Irish blood in me by the Griffins, but the Carews were French. Anyway, I wish there was not a drop of Irish blood in my veins."

"So do I, from my heart," said Farrell; but, re-membering his family at home, said no more.

" Now, the wisest and best thing for you to do, Farrell," said Ryan, " is to move off as soon as you can. How long, Ned, did my attorney say we could give them?"

" Three days, sir," answered Ned.

" And you *are* bent on doing this?" said Farrell, wringing his hands.

" My dear man," said Ryan calmly, " I sent for you for a little quiet chat this morning, intending to mention this matter to you in the course of the conversation; and now you lose your temper."

So saying, Ryan stepped nimbly into the office, for both were outside at this time, and quickly closed and locked the door. Miles had been wait-ing outside for his neighbor, and both slowly re-turned home, a pair of heart-broken men.

CHAPTER V.

SOME MORE OF THE DOINGS OF THIS VERY HONEST MAN

HE evening following the morning of her father's interview with John G. Ryan, Annie was sitting alone in the shade of a tall whitethorn which grew near the river's bank, her head bent on her bosom, and the warm tears streaming down her pale cheeks. Herself and her mother had spent a morning of the most intense anxiety, dreading, hoping, and praying for good tidings, and guarding lest Francis would notice anything unusual the matter; for they were resolved to keep the sad news from him as long as possible.

The anguish of the family was intense when Farrell returned with word that their worst fears were realized—in less than three days they would be without a home. Mrs. Reilly fainted in her unhappy husband's arms, and was with great difficulty restored to consciousness. Francis—it was needless to keep the calamity from his knowledge now—was so oppressed with grief that he cried like a child. Poor Annie bore up the

best of any, and did all in her power to comfort
her father and mother, and insisted on them all
joining her in a rosary for assistance to come
through this terrible misfortune that had befallen
them. After prayers, they felt considerably relieved, and set about the best way of removing
their valuables to some temporary place of security.

Annie had struggled so hard to repress her
feelings during the day that, when evening came,
she felt she must give vent to her tears, or
her heart would break. So overwhelming was
the misfortune that she could not bear up
against it all day—the desolation of her own
home, and Ryan's threat against her lover. When
her father and brother were silently engaged,
she left the cottage, and betook herself to the
spot where James used to sing to her. With
what a light, bounding heart she used to approach this cosey place! But this evening how
different! James was always there waiting for
her; but this evening the seat was empty. She
went up the hillside a little distance, to obtain a
better view along the shore; but, no—far as
her eye could reach, he was nowhere to be seen.
For a little she stood on the hillside in the
calm summer air, her eyes strained in the direction from which he approached the seat every

evening, till her heart sank with disappointment, and her sight grew dim; then she mechanically sought the spot, and let fall her burning tears.

"Oh!" thought she, "if, in addition to our misfortune, Ryan has already put his threat into execution against James, and he is dragged away to where I may never see him again, what shall I do? Oh!" exclaimed she, raising her hands to heaven, "if such has happened, may God in His mercy take me!"

She then bowed her head and wept, she knew not how long, till she was startled by hearing a well-known voice pronounce her name; but, before she could raise her head, James O'Rourke was seated by her side, her hand clasped firmly in his. Annie turned her streaming face towards him. For a moment neither spoke. O'Rourke's lips quivered, and his whole frame shook, but he heroically kept back the tears rising to his eyes.

He had made his appearance so suddenly, and the poor girl's joy was so great, that she could only cry the more and press the hand that held hers. At length James said:

"Annie, it's no use in me asking you the cause of those tears. I already know the misfortune that has befallen us all. But it is useless now to pine and give way to sorrow. Better bear up bravely, as I know you will, Annie, when you come to reflect. The calamity is sudden, and we must be quick to meet it."

" Oh! it is a dreadful thing, James," said Annie. " I struggled with my feelings for my father and mother's sake. It is only since I came here I have showed such signs of grief."

" And Heaven bless you for coming here this evening," said he. " I would have been here long ago, if I could; I have had a busy evening of it."

Annie surveyed him more closely, and noticed how soiled and mud-spattered his clothing was, and that his face was torn with thorns and brambles.

" James," said she wildly, the recollection of Ryan's threat again rushing into her head, " in God's name, tell me what has happened. Has Ryan—"

" Exactly, Annie," said he. " I see you know it."

" Father told us," said she, " that he made some threat against you; and that has grieved me more than anything else."

" God bless you!" said James, placing his arm around her neck. " I feel his villany more for your sake; I knew it would grieve you. He *has* put his threat into execution. They are after me now."

Annie's head fell against his shoulder, and she moaned deeply.

"Oh! now I am sorry I have told you so much," said her lover, raising her head, and looking into the beautiful, pale, quivering face. "But now let me tell you more. You promise, Annie, now, you promise," and he pressed his lips to hers, "that you will be a brave girl, as you always were? This misery will soon be over."

"Oh! yes, I do promise," said she; "but I beg of you to tell me quickly whatever it is."

"God bless you, my darling," said he; and again he kissed her. "I rely on you, Annie; you are as brave as a little lion, now that your resolution is taken. Well, Ryan ' the Pig ' (John was known by this nickname amongst the peasantry), not satisfied with driving us from house and home, has taken it into his head to make a charge to the police against me. What the nature of the accusation is I know no more of than you do; but he actually swore something against me; for my poor father—God help him!—saw the warrant. When the police were in our house a few hours ago, I happened by good luck to be absent at the time; and now they are searching the whole neighborhood for me. My father managed to give me word in time to elude them, and requested

me, if possible, to return to the house as soon as
I could, and he would try and procure money
enough to send me to America. I did so, and
he gave me those seven sovereigns. He wanted
me to take a few more he had, but I would not.
He will need all that can be spared."

"O James!" said Annie, and her hand trembled violently in his. "And you are going?"

"You promised to be a brave little girl, Annie,"
replied he, kissing her fervently. "Listen to me.
They will surely return after nightfall, in the hope
of finding me there; and for your sake, Annie,
and for the sake of my poor old father, I must
disappoint them. Night is closing around now.
We have not long to stay; and again I ask you
to promise you will bear up bravely and gaily
till we meet again."

"Ah, James!" said the poor girl, and her little
hand felt as cold as ice, "till we meet again.
When will that be, James?"

"In God's good time; and that will be very
soon, my love," replied he. "I know I shall
get on well in America; and how I shall perse-
vere, having such an object to work for—to bring
you to me, my darling! Nothing shall deter me;
and your innocent, sweet prayers will save me
from every danger."

Both were silent for a moment. The grass

around them was wet with dew; the thick mist began to envelope the bosom of the river; the mountain-top was no longer visible. The eastern horizon was beginning to assume a golden hue, and it was evident the moon would soon rise.

"Annie," said James, looking cautiously around, "the time has come. I thank God I am not bidding you farewell; but I must bid you good-by, my love, for a few weeks. How swiftly our weeks at school fled away! But those few now will look like so many years to me. But they, too, will have an end, and then we will be together again."

Annie *was* a brave little girl. When he held both her hands in his, and looked into her face in the dim light, she was ashy pale; but not a tear fell. A sad smile came on her lips; and when he pressed her to his breast, and again and again kissed her, she did not add to the anguish of that moment by a sob. And when he darted away in the darkness, and left her alone on the strand, she knelt down and besought Heaven to watch over him.

CHAPTER VI.

THE CHARGE AGAINST JAMES O'ROURKE EX-
PLAINED. A VISIT TO AN IRISH MAGIS-
TRATE.

OHN G. RYAN was a very cautious
and a very prudent man. When he
observed so many of nature's laws
so faithfully, it is needless to say he
was not unmindful of the first—self-preservation.
Miles O'Rourke or his son had never done him
an injury, and, prominently as he shone among
other men, they hardly ever mentioned his name
or bestowed a thought on him. In fact, Miles
and his son belonged to that sensible class of
people who mind their own business and let the
virtues and failings of their neighbors alone.
Ryan knew he was about to perpetrate a grievous
wrong upon them, and James being a spirited
young fellow, he dreaded he might be revenged
upon him. This consideration annoyed Ryan
considerably for a little time, but for a little time
only. In the recesses of his cunning brain he
soon hit upon a remedy.

He was sitting in his arm-chair in his shirt-
sleeves as usual, biting the ends of his chin
whisker, and pondering over the vexed question,
when a light suddenly shone upon him, and he
jumped up with a loud " By golly, sir !" that
made the crooked-eyed youth jump also, and his
eyes jump, too, in a ludicrous manner.

" I have hit upon it !" exclaimed Ryan, sitting
down again, and slapping his knee ; but as he did
not look towards the wondering youth, the latter
did not venture to speak.

" Ned," said Ryan at length, turning to his
charming clerk, " I want you to swear something
for me."

" Anything you like, sir," replied Ned, half
standing up.

" You're a splendid fellow, Ned," said he .
" you and I *will* get along smoothly when we lay
our names together."

The comely youth grinned from ear to ear,
and turned a whole battery of blinks on his kind
master.

" Ned," said Ryan, stretching his legs, " do you
know Miles O'Rourke's son ? "

" Yes, sir," replied Ned ; " as well as I know
myself, sir."

" So far, all right," said Ryan. " When have
you seen him last ? "

" I met him and three other fellows on the road three or four nights ago," was the answer.

" You must be particular as to dates," said Ryan, shaking his head : " say three nights ago. Now, I want you—"

" Yes, sir," broke in the ardent youth.

" Listen to me," said Ryan, with a slight frown. " Now, I want you to make an affidavit before a magistrate that you were concealed behind a hedge at the time you saw O'Rourke and those other chaps, and that you heard them planning to rob the police barracks of the arms there. Go back to your writing now, and I'll call you again when I am prepared to go with you before the magistrate."

Ned grinned again and again—something so very unusual for him that the work must have delighted him beyond measure.

Ryan, having transacted his morning's business, talked, lied, and cheated as usual—in fact, brought into play a great many of his qualities—at length called Ned to accompany him to the office of the dispenser of law and justice. Now, the private office of an Irish country magistrate is such a very private, sacred spot that some of our readers may not object to accompany the mighty John, the proud Ned, and our humble self into the presence of Richard Seraife, Esq., J.P., on this occasion

Richard Scruffy, Esq., J.P., was a very fair type of the Irish J.P. some years ago, or, in fact. would not be altogether out of fashion to-day. Short and stout in figure, with an immense red face, small forehead, and very bald head, an expression of haughty contempt, tinged with a shade of profound knowledge, slowly moving in terrible waves across his countenance, he looked the very picture of stern, unbending justice.

He wore a blue body-coat, wide in the skirts, and very tight in the shoulders · wide trowsers, white as snow, save one large discolored spot on one thigh, the smell of which, taken in conjunction with the high color of his face, might lead a malicious person to imagine something he had no right to ; a long, wide vest, which seemed to bę in open rebellion with the rest of his attire, so fierce, staring, and puckered was it ; and an immense black neck-cloth.

The apartment in which he sat was of very small dimensions—four like Richard Scruffy, Esq., J.P., would fill it to overflowing. It contained, besides Richard—he always sat there at least half the day, knowing vigilance is one of Justice's handmaids—a little round table with very dirty legs, one gigantic chair, and a row of shelving filled with large law-books, these latter looking so very dry that one wondered how any sensible insurance company could be induced to give a policy on them. The large chair served two purposes: first, it served as a judicial bench; and, secondly, as a bed for the justice; for, not having much business on hand, being supported by a stipend, Richard slept just as often as Justice did, and often she found it no very easy matter to rouse him up. When that impartial goddess, in the double shape of John G. Ryan and Ned Buttler, articled clerk of the aforesaid John, came to the office door, and when Ryan struck the door thrice with his knuckles and once with his foot, and then put his ear to the keyhole, the only response was the slow, regular snore of Richard within. Ryan scratched his head, and, looking round at Ned, said :

"Here's a fix. What am I to do?"

"Dunt the door again, sir," was the prompt reply.

"I don't know about that," said Ryan, looking somewhat in dread; "he has such a bad temper, if we were to rouse him up suddenly, he might get so mad that he'd clear us both out. I'll stand back by the wall there, and do you come here to the door, and give a rap or two."

Ned quickly changed places with his master and gave the door two such knocks that Ryan

raised his eyes, hands, and heels at the same time
Ned listened ; still no answer.

" Try it again," said Ryan, in a heavy whisper,
which could be heard much further away than his
loudest call : "this time with your foot."

Ryan's eye caught a glimpse of Ned's heel as
it swung behind him. The next moment a loud
crash sounded on his ears, followed by the noise
of something falling inside, and then a stifled
voice within the office called out,

" Murder ! Housebreaking ! Where am I ? "

Ryan knew the magistrate's voice, and retreated
as far as the gate, where he stood with his head
just inside the entrance, and by numerous excited
gestures and heavy whispers directed the equally
alarmed Ned to speak.

" Who are you, you scoundrel ? " again demanded the voice.

" Speak," exclaimed Ryan, bending down and
lifting a large paving-stone, " or I'll scatter your
brains against the wall."

" It's me, sir," said Ned, in a husky voice, and
turning his head towards Ryan.

" Let him hear you," said the latter, holding
the stone in a very threatening attitude. " Say
it's a man to do his *duty*, according to the
law."

" Where is my vagabond servant ? Where are

my pistols? Is there no one to come to my relief?" said the voice inside.

"It's a man according to the law," said Ned, "and wants to see you badly, sir. We're here this hour."

"You're a nice man to mention the name of the law," said the voice, "and come here and conduct yourself like a burglar, which I have no doubt you are."

"Say: Your honor, we only want to speak with you a minute or two," said Ryan.

"Our honors only want to speak with you a minute or two," said Ned, in his excitement.

A pause followed, during which John shook the stone ominously at Ned, and pledged himself to straighten the eyes in his head, if he did nothing else.

At length Ned heard a footstep enter the office from some other apartment within the building, and then he could hear the angry voice of the magistrate while he rated his servant for his want of vigilance.

At length Richard Scruffy, Esq., told the man, in a very loud voice, to open the door. Ned cast a terrified look on Ryan, who gave him such a savage glance in return that it completely turned him round. The key sounded in the door.

"Stand your ground," whispered Ryan, "or I'll knock—"

The door was pulled open, and Ned's eyes danced around the apartment, and, alighting on Mr. Scruffy's indignant face, performed a regular "break-down."

"Will I bring him in, sir?" asked the servant.

"Oh! no," replied the magistrate, shading his face; "let him come no nearer to me. He looks like the devil. Ask him what he wants. I wish a few of the police were here now."

Ned stood still just outside the door, his cap squeezed into a lump in his hand, and kept up a galling, incessant fire of blinks on the magistrate.

"What's your business with his honor?" demanded the servant, in a very haughty voice, and assuming a very threatening attitude; for Ned, as our readers already know, was anything but a strong man.

"He'll tell you all," said Ned, in desperation, and pointing towards Ryan who had advanced his head a little further, to catch what was being said. The servant glanced towards him, and Ryan seeing he could delay no longer, began to approach the door.

"This is another of them, sir," said the servant; "but I think, sir, this last fellow is a tradesman of the town."

Richard Scruffy, Esq., stretched his neck to look into the yard, and, seeing Ryan smiled, but quickly made up his mind to be stern, as became the majesty of the law; so he frowned grandly, but not exactly on Ryan.

"Your honor," said the latter, with such a tremendous bow that his foot slipped on the pavement, and he fell against the side of the door, and his hat tumbled into the office. Ryan's hat was always unfortunate, and gave him so much trouble that we wonder a man of his wisdom did not conclude to go bareheaded. "P—p—pa—par—pardon me, sir," he stammered, as he regained his balance, "I—I—I—"

"You overdid the thing," said Richard, with a sore attempt at a smile; but quickly added, while his judicial brow lowered, "Do you know that fellow?" pointing to Ned. "He is a decidedly roguish-looking fellow. He'll get the gallows yet, or my name is not R. Scruffy. How is it he says you know all about him?"

"I took hold of him," said Ryan, approaching familiarly.

"Don't dirty the floor with your feet," exclaimed Richard, stamping one of his own on the boards. "Go outside, sir, and wipe them, sir, and stand by the door while you are talking to me, sir."

" Anything at all your honor plazes," said Ryan bursting outside. " I beg your pardon, sir."

" And another thing I beg to remind you of," said Richard, in a lofty voice, and fitting on his spectacles: " don't bother me with an account of your rascals. You are the leader of a dangerous crowd." And offended justice climbed into the big chair, and dipped its pen into a huge inkstand.

John, not knowing but that terrible pen would indite some words that might ruin him, mounted the door-step, and exclaimed, while the heavy sweat stood on his brow, " Your honor knows me as a loyal, rebel-hating man."

" Confine yourself to the case," roared the magistrate, " or "— turning to the servant—" you put him outside the gate." The fellow moved to John's side.

" I will, your honor," said Ryan. " I came here to your honor to-day, and brought my young man, in the interest of her Majesty the Queen."

" Go on," said the magistrate.

" My boy, yer honor, seen and heerd a crowd of rebels plannin'—"

" Stop, sir!" exclaimed the magistrate. " I'll swear the boy; bring him here."

The servant guided Ned into the office, and planted him in front of the magistrate.

" Don't you interrupt, on your peril," said the

latter, looking over his spectacles at Ryan. Ryan backed a little nearer the door.

The book being handed to Ned, he instantly kissed it. Mr. Scruffy looked at him for fully a minute, to Ned's great comfort, and then said :

" That fellow is a fool ; I don't think I can take his evidence. What do you think ?"—this to the servant.

" More knave nor fool," replied that personage.

" He's greedy in the good cause, your honor," said Ryan, while something painful struggled in his neck. " Wait, Ned, ye ——, till his honor says the word."

Ned did wait this time, and related the story to the magistrate in, as near as he could remember, the words his master had told him. Richard's rage knew no bounds.

" They " (the gentry, we suppose) " were standing on a volcano which, if it were not quenched with a flood of law, would burst forth and scorch up society itself. Young, man, and you, Ryan— though you did dirty the floor—the Queen of this realm is indebted to you two," said Richard Scruffy, Esq., as he commenced to make out the warrant for young O'Rourke's arrest, " and shall, through me, her servant, hear of your exertions on her behalf."

Ryan's joy knew no bounds.

"Your honor," said he, scratching his head, "I don't know what to do with myself. I don't know how to express my thanks. I am sure we—"

"Put them out; clear the office," said the magistrate, with calm, cold dignity.

CHAPTER VII.

LEAVING THE OLD HOME.

HEN Annie, with tired limbs and sad, sick heart, returned to the cottage after parting from her lover, she found her father and brother putting their valuables in a condition for removal to a friend's house some miles distant. Farrell had resolved that they would not wait till the bailiff came to dispossess them, but would move away before suffering the indignity of being turned out by that obnoxious official. Owing to their unhappy state, they did not notice the deep grief exhibited in Annie's face. She set herself to help them in their work at once, calmly, quietly; and, after a little, no one could tell that any other pain lay at her heart except grief for the desolation that had fallen on her poor father's home.

Love, when shrouded with sorrow, is often a strange feeling. It lies silently gnawing at the heart, but shows itself not to the world. Although Annie's face had grown pale and wasted during that night, in the morning she seemed the happiest one of the family—if we can apply the word happy to that stricken home.

Early in the day, Farrell and his son had everything ready. All the neighbors came to their assistance; for no man in the parish was more deservedly popular than Farrell Reilly. His ready help to others in their hour of need was not forgotten when his own trouble came.

It was drawing towards the close of summer, and Farrell had as much of his crop as the season permitted gathered in. A number of men, with horses and carts, and everything available for carrying a load, thronged to the little farm. The cattle Francis had driven in the early part of the day to the friend's farm, and by evening everything that could be removed was taken away.

Farrell, and his wife, and Annie stood by the old cottage, looking after the last load of furniture as it lumbered down the hillside. Mrs. Reilly had been very ill all the day, and the family dreaded very much the effect of the last moment upon her. Farrell and she had lived happily in the old place for over twenty years. Her own family home stood on the top of an adjoining hill looking down on her husband's cottage. Her father and mother had died some years before, and bad crops and sickness had swept away every member of the family. One of her brothers died

from hardships endured by hard work in the cold,
wet season. Another had left for America many
years before, and the only account she ever heard
of him was that he had died of yellow fever in
Savannah. Still, it was a melancholy pleasure to
Mrs. Reilly to sit in the little garden during the
long summer evenings with her knitting, while
the rest of the family were engaged elsewhere, and
turn her eyes towards her father's house, now un-
tenanted, and gaze on its ivy-covered walls and
tall, bare chimneys, which seemed to speak to her
of times long gone. Then she would think of her
childhood days, when she laughed, and sported,
and played on the hill-top. Every tree, bush, or
rock called back to her memory some recollection
of those days. Then she would think of the time
when Farrell, a gay young fellow, with a bright,
laughing face, used to come and sit by her as she
milked the cows in the little sheltered corner
field. How she used to delight in annoying him
by calling him names, and mocking his old frieze
coat, with one new arm, and his old slouch hat,
with the piece of black cloth wrong side out
sewed on its front with white thread. How she
used to refuse to let him help her in any way, but
rebuff him in every way; and then, when he was
gone, cry till her eyes grew red for saying so much
to him, and make a resolution never to torment

him again—a resolution which was sure to be
broken the following evening. Then of the evening when Farrell, in spite of all her efforts, insisted on carrying the milk-cans a little way for
her, and how very sheepish and red he looked
when he left them down behind the garden-gate,
and, turning his eyes away from hers, began to
fumble the pockets of his coat, and asked her to
speak a word with him. How, when he asked
her would she become his wife, and began telling
her how snug and happy he could keep her, how
she ran away from him, and told him she thought
him a bigger fool than ever; that night she cried
till her heart was sick. How poor Farrell came
the following evening, and she would not speak
to him nor look at him for some time. How
Farrell carried the milk-cans for her that evening
again, and begged of her to let him ask her father
and mother for their consent; and how delighted
he was when she told him she did not care, till
she had to knock the hat off his head, and tell
him to keep a proper distance. Even then she
could not help laughing at the awkward embar-
rassment of Farrell; and how every word stuck
in his throat when he came around the following
Sunday night, right gaily clad, with a bottle of
whisky staring out of each pocket, to make the
request. Then she would think of what a good

kind husband Farrell had always been. If her
thoughts came down to the time when her poor
brothers, after every effort, failed to keep the old
homestead, the tears would fill her eyes, and she
would re-enter the cottage.

As we said before, Farrell, and his son and
daughter, seeing her distress of mind, and knowing how fondly she loved the dear old spot, were
in great dread lest the final moment would prove
too much for her. Farrell allowed his son to go
on, while he and Annie tried to engage the poor
woman's thoughts by talking of the great kindness of their neighbors, and how well and neatly
everything was prepared for the journey.

"You see," said Farrell, raising his hat from his
eyes, where he had kept it all the morning, and
looking round on his wife and daughter, "the
kindness and honest generosity of our neighbors
altogether take away the bitterness of this day.
Surely it is true 'tis only in adversity we can tell
our friends. And," added he, with an attempt
at a smile, "in our misfortune, we cannot count
our friends. We seem to have no enemies at
all."

"None but the *one*, Farrell," said Mrs. Reilly,
looking at him with a strange, wan, wild look,
"and can all the friends in the world make up
what he has done? Heaven forgive me!" she

added sorrowfully. "Sure our best friend is God."

"Just think of that, now," said Farrell. He was going to say more, but a scream from Annie startled him, and, turning round, he saw his wife reclining in her daughter's arms, while a stream of blood poured from her nose and down over her face and breast. Farrell took her in his arms, and, handing Annie the key, bade her open the door again; for, unobserved by Mrs. Reilly, he had locked the door, never again intending to cross the threshold of the cottage. The alarmed girl did so, and, procuring some water in an old vessel which had been thrown aside, poured it over the face and hands of the fainting woman. Everything they could do was fruitless to stop the flow of blood; and, terribly alarmed, and almost dead from grief, Farrell told Annie to run for the priest. Her hair flowing in wild disorder, and her cheeks wet from tears, Annie started off to the chapel. She found Father Fitzpatrick walking around the church reading. The clergyman had raised his eyes from the book when she was entering the gate, and, seeing the wild and alarmed-looking girl coming towards him, advanced to meet her. Seeing who it was, he asked:

"Annie, my child, what is the matter?"

She stopped short, and for a second or two could make no reply.

"What is wrong with you, my child?" he asked again softly, laying his hand on her shoulder.

"O father!" said Annie at length, "I fear mother is dying. Pray, father, come quickly to the house with me."

The good priest needed no second request, but, hastening into the chapel, prepared himself for the solemn visit. Annie waited for him at his request, and, his car being quickly harnessed, both dashed away at full speed to—to—where was once the home of Farrell Reilly.

CHAPTER VIII.

LEAVING THE OLD HOME.

HEN Father Fitzpatrick and Annie reached the cottage, they found Mrs. Reilly still insensible; but the flow of blood from her nose had been stopped. As they drove up the hillside, the clergyman looked with a serious, troubled face at the cottage, with its bare and desolated appearance, broken panes, and closed door; then at the little farmyard, in which little heaps of rubbish were lying here and there; but everything else was gone. He sighed heavily, but made no remark to Annie.

Mrs. Reilly reclined against her husband's breast as he sat on the ground by the wall.

"O father dear!" said Farrell, as the priest entered, "I am afraid she is going from us. I knew this would be too much for her. See how deadly pale she is; and I cannot feel her breath."

The clergyman bent down, and lifted one of

the suffering woman's hands in his, and felt her pulse.

" Her pulse is very low, Farrell," said he. " She is certainly very much exhausted. Let me assist you to bring her to the door. She will recover quicker in the open air than here."

Both carried her to the door-step, and Farrell supported her in his arms, while the priest chafed her hands and temples.

Annie's grief knew no bounds. She could not silence her sobs, and, as in her present state she could be of no service to her mother, the priest requested her to keep within the house. This poor Annie could not do, but stood apart wringing her hands and moaning sadly.

At length the clergyman announced that the sufferer's pulse beat more lively, and that she would soon recover.

" Oh ! thank heaven, father," said Annie, approaching and peering into her mother's face. " Do you think truly she will recover ?"

" With God's help, my child," returned he, " I think she will recover sufficiently to—"

He stopped suddenly; and Annie and her father looked into his anxious, gentle face. Farrell well knew what the father would have added, and, raising his eyes to heaven, exclaimed, in a voice that went to the kind priest's heart :

"Lord, look down on us to-day! We are indeed but poor outcasts."

Gradually the fingers of the hand Father Fitzpatrick held in his began to move, the white lips parted a little, the poor woman opened her eyes for an instant, and, seeming to notice the priest, she faintly uttered:

"Thanks be to God!"

After a few moments, her eyes opened again, and she looked around on the little group.

"Speak to me, Mary. One word to poor me," said Farrell, putting the side of his face to hers— "one word."

"Oh! that is you, Farrell," said she. "Where are we?"

"We are here in the old home yet," said he.

"Yet, Farrell," said she, in a voice so low and weak as to be hardly audible, "I thought Annie and I were on board a very large ship going to America, and that you were beyond waiting for us."

"Father Fitzpatrick is here, Mary," said her husband gently.

"Oh! and he was in my dream, too," said Mrs. Reilly.

"Thank God and His Holy Mother you have recovered!" said the priest, again lifting her

hand; " that your life has been spared this time
You will soon be well again. I will wait a little
till you are beyond danger ; but I think 'tis not
necessary to administer to you."

" Oh ! thank you a thousand times for that,
father," said Annie, in a whisper. " You being
here will keep her from thinking of our downfall
till we are away from this place."

" Away from this place ? " said the priest, with
a startled look.

" Oh ! yes, father ; Ryan put us out. But don't
mention it now," looking at her mother ; " father
will explain all to you. We are moving to my
cousin's house, and must leave here to-night.
Everything belonging to us is gone."

The good priest's heart sank within him. The
oldest and most respectable family in his parish
banished so ruthlessly. What would follow next ?
He thought of the *blessings* of the union, and resolved to join the National Association as soon
as expedient.

Mrs. Reilly's strength continued to return
slowly ; and the kind, gentle priest entered into
a quiet conversation with her on the improvements he was making in his new church ; told
her how beautiful the altar of the Blessed Virgin
would look when completed.

" Were it not for the devotion of yourself and

some other good ladies of the parish, in decorat-
ing it with flowers," he went on, " it would have
looked very poorly indeed during the month of
May devotions.   But now we will soon have a
new altar, with candlesticks from Paris; and the
' Virgin and Child' which we had then will be
too small, so I am going up to Dublin in a few
days to purchase an elegant one, and you must
come and give me your opinion of it before we
set it up; and then those two windows on each
side of the altar are going to be taken out.   A
wealthy Irish-American gentleman, a namesake
of mine, whom I met on his way to the lakes a
few days ago, is going to put in beautiful stained
glass in its place; so that I think, when everything is completed, we'll not have'much right to
feel ashamed of our little chapel."

The kind, affectionate manner and chat of the
good pastor soothed so much the anguish the
poor woman felt that it almost made her forget
her desolation for the time.   He continued to
engage her thoughts in this manner till he saw
she was strong enough to be assisted into his car
and taken to her new home.   Farrell and Annie
thanked him fervently for his kind proposition;
the four seated themselves in the car, and, as they
did so, the priest began relating a comic incident
about one of his parishoners, whom the others

knew very well, which he kept up till they were out of view of the cottage. If he saw any signs of the return of the deep sorrow they had felt in the face of any of his companions, he instantly be-spoke that one's attention, and talked and laugh-ed incessantly till they reached the house of Maurice Handley, which was their destination. After again receiving their heartfelt thanks, and giving them his blessing, Father Fitzpatrick re-turned home with as sad a heart as those he had parted from.

CHAPTER IX.

AURICE HANDLEY, Farrell's nephew, lived in a cosey little cottage a short way from the broad road and close by the demesne wall of Castlesaunderson, the Irish residence of Colonel Saunderson, the gentleman who had sold the town-land containing Reilly and O'Rourke's farms to Ryan and Crofton. He, too, was a tenant of Saunderson's. Maurice was a young man of thirty or thereabouts, and only a year married. His wife was a strong, healthy young woman, with an abundance of black hair and a very sharp, rather unfriendly face. A small fruit of their union, in the shape of a pretty little girl about six weeks old, had already appeared, and Maurice was very happy. But the sudden desolation that had fallen on his uncle had pained him very much. His mother had died a few years before, and Maurice was very much attached to her, and used to listen with pride and pleasure to her stories about the old home.

Father Fitzpatrick, before leaving, had caution-

ed him and his wife to be careful and mention
nothing relating to the misfortune that had befallen his uncle's family in the hearing of Mrs.
Reilly, but to talk over other matters, and appear
as gay as possible. Both thanked the good priest
for his advice, and promised to strictly obey his
instructions. Francis and Annie, too, entered
into the plot, and, hard as the effort was, conducted themselves as they used to do in the old home
before sorrow came there. The nephew, in order
to carry out the plan to the fullest, resolved to
make their first evening one of rejoicing, and
procured the necessary articles from the village
for that purpose.

Mrs. Handley and Annie set out for the shop
together, and, now that she was from the presence
of her heart-broken parents, and had one of her
own sex to confide in, her tears began to fall, and
she lamented bitterly their sad situation. Mrs.
Handley's only effort to comfort her was by reminding her that she saw no cause for her lamenting now that she had found a home so quickly,
and added that many whom she had known to be
" put out " had no friends to open their door to
them, but let them go to the poor-house.

"Oh!" said Annie, looking surprised through
her tears at the cutting words of the other, "I
don't think we are so far reduced as to be com-

pelled to go to the poor-house. Father has a little left yet."

"No danger of him or you either going there while Maurice has a home. That man thinks more of his friends than I believe is good for him. Whatever your father has got, he can hold on to it now."

Annie's face flushed, and her eye kindled; this cold taunting in the day of her distress she could not be silent under.

"Martha," she replied, drying her tears, "had we known how unwelcome we were to you, we could very easily have found a home with some of our neighbors."

"Oh! I didn't intend to vex you at all," replied Martha, with a toss of her head. "For my part, you are welcome to stay here as long as you like."

"We will not trouble you long," replied Annie. "I shall tell my brother, and he will provide some place for us. You may rely on it."

The two then walked on in silence, Martha amusing herself with humming a verse of an old country ballad. Maurice was all kindness and hospitality, and succeeded so well in entertaining the old pair that evening that, before they parted for the night, both felt much happier than they had at any time since their desolation. When the others were engaged, Annie beckoned Francis to follow her, and when he did so, led him to the edge of the grove, and, sitting down on the grass, addressed him thus:

" Francis, I have tried hard to keep my feelings from my father and mother this evening."

" That was a great effort on my part, too," replied Francis.

" Oh! but, Francis," she said, "you don't know as much as I do. By Maurice's wife we are heartily unwelcome here. I had a few words with her on our way to the village this evening. She insulted me very badly." And Annie put her apron to her eyes and began to cry.

" Oh! nonsense, Annie," said Francis, drying her tears; " tell me what has passed. I could see it in her to-night by the way she looked at father and mother, and kept continually finding an excuse to make one or the other shift their place at the fire, that we were anything but welcome. But then, Maurice is such a generous-hearted fellow himself I would rather not notice this for awhile, till we can find some little place of our own."

" Not for the world," said Annie, " would I let mother know of it. I hope she has not noticed it herself already. She would sooner lie in this wood at night than there, if she once thought we were unwelcome."

"I'll tell you, Annie," said Francis, after a short pause, "what I intend doing. Colonel Saunderson has lately built a number of small cottages, which he intends filling with his workmen ; and I am thinking of seeking work at the castle and, if I obtain it and one of those little houses, we will be somewhat independent again."

"Ah! Francis, that is a good thought," said Annie ; "but I fear it would break poor mother's heart living amongst such people as her neighbors then would be. And then, you a workman at the castle."

"I have thought of all that," said Francis. "When mother reflects, I don't think she will take it so bad after all. Along with what little we have got, I could soon earn enough to bring us to America. I could not think of leaving them, now that they have nothing only my exertions to rely on."

"Francis," said Annie earnestly, "what do you think of this? I cannot be of much service to you here—none at all, in fact ; only a burden. And now, if you think father could spare enough to send me to America alone, I could earn enough there to be of great help to you."

"Ah! I am afraid they would never consent to

you crossing the ocean alone," said Francis.
" For my part, I know very well you would suc-
ceed. I wish you had thought of this when
James O'Rourke was going; but," he added,
"you couldn't easily have done that. It would
not have been very pleasant to be under the protection of a man in the danger poor James was in."

Francis felt the hand he held in his tremble,
and, looking around, he saw Annie struggling to
keep back her tears.

"Well, well, Annie," said he, with a smile, "I
shouldn't have spoken of James to you now; but
you know he succeeded in getting off safely, so
that he is now beyond danger, and you and he may
meet on the other side of the water some day. I
have it now, my girl," and he slapped the back
of her hand. "I would bet a sovereign, if I had
it, that your whole anxiety to get to America
is because James O'Rourke is there." And he
laughed and shook her by the hair.

" No, indeed, Francis," said she; "you do me
wrong there. I should certainly be glad to meet
him or any other friend in a strange country;
but my whole anxiety is to be able to assist you
at home."

"I didn't doubt you, Annie," said he. "You
must pardon what I have said. You are a great
good girl and a wise girl— "

"Well, well, now, Francis," said she, interrupting him, "mother will get alarmed if we stay here much longer; and so let us decide on what to do. After what passed this evening, you would not ask your sister to remain in that woman's house; and I beg of you to help me to make father and mother let me go. Mother will not be so hard to induce as you think. Nancy Brady had a letter from her daughter Kitty a couple of weeks ago, and showed it to mother. It gave a splendid account of New York, and contained five pounds and a promise of five more before the end of summer. You know mother always liked Kitty, and would not have the least doubt of anything she'd say. Now, if I got along as well as Kitty, I could have you with me before three months, and surely both of us could keep the old pair comfortably at home if they would rather live here."

"Oh! Annie, how can I plead with them to let you go away from us? But sure, I see the truth of every word you say."

"God bless you, Francis!" said she. "We will go back and say no more about it to-night; but delay is useless, you know, so we will try them to-morrow evening."

CHAPTER X.

"MY NATIVE LAND, GOOD-NIGHT!"

—*Byron.*

ARRELL REILLY and his wife were a very common-sense couple; none of those sentimental people who sit down and weep and mourn over misfortune, and close their eyes to every effort at overcoming it. They saw something must be done, and done quickly; and, painful and distressing as it was to them, the plan for the future laid down by their son and daughter met their approval much easier than the latter had expected. Mrs. Reilly wept bitterly for some minutes, and poor Farrell wrung his hands and paced up and down the floor a few times; then, turning to Annie, who tried to wear as cheerful a face as she could, he said:

"In God's name, my child, I'll make no objection."

"Nor I, Annie," said her mother. "I will beseech Heaven, night and day, to watch over you, and the just and merciful God will one day, I hope, allow us to see your face again."

It is needless to dwell on the incidents of the few days spent in Annie's preparation for her journey. She went to confession to the good Father Fitzpatrick, and told him of her intention, and received his blessing and a promise that he would say a Mass for her safety while on the wide ocean.

The night previous to her departure soon came, and a number of the friends of the family assembled at Maurice Handley's to take farewell of Annie and bid her Godspeed on her journey. Mrs. Reilly was seated on a chair, on one side of the room, her head resting on her hand, watching Annie and Francis packing up the little trunk, and Farrell stood by the window, looking out on the road, when the first visitor, Nancy Brady, called upon them. She carried a small bundle in her hand containing some linen and worsted, and a bunch of green shamrock, which she intended sending with Annie to her daughter in America. The brother and sister were right glad to see her, and gave her a warm welcome ; for they knew all she had to say in praise of America would help to console their mother for the evening.

Nancy was a poor widow, and lived in a small cabin by the wayside, a little distance from the old home of Reilly. After the death of her husband, and when she was left with her little girl in extreme poverty, Farrell Reilly had been a good friend to her, often supplying her for months with provisions, when otherwise her child and herself might have perished of want. It grieved the poor old lady sorely, the misfortune that had befallen her benefactor and his family. Her cabin-door commanded a view of the cottage, and, when the family were gone, she built up the door on that side, and opened another on the opposite end of the cabin. The moment she entered Handley's and saw Mrs. Reilly, she smiled as if she felt quite happy, and, seating herself by her side, began to praise their good wisdom in sending Annie to America.

"My poor daughter," she went on, "that had neither education nor much ability of any kind, see how well she is doing. Since she went to America, I have never known the want of a shilling. And your daughter, Mrs. Reilly, the best scholar—as Mr. Lacy often told me—at his school, and so smart in every way, how is *she* going to get along?"

Mrs. Reilly said very little, but let the good-hearted creature talk on in this strain. The effect of what she was saying, however, was not lost on the other, and she soon felt well enough to assist Mrs. Brady and Annie in completing the trunk.

Amongst those who came to bid the girl farewell were a number of young men, sons of the
neighboring farmers, most of whom one day intended taking the same course. These in particular laid themselves out to enliven the party
and spend a pleasant night. Annie's health and
prosperity were drunk a hundred times. Numerous songs were sung, mostly patriotic, or bearing
on the event which assembled them together.

Thus the night passed away, and morning
came. None of the family went to sleep; for, by
the time the last of those who were going no
further than the house had left, it was time for
Annie, and those who intended leaving her at the
railway station, to depart, too.

As the time for her parting from her daughter
approached, Mrs. Reilly felt her heart growing
doubly sad, and she dreaded she would break
down at the last moment. The state of her
health did not permit her to leave the house.
Nancy tried to engage her attention now more
than ever.

At length Annie went into the room to put
on her hat. Noticing this, her mother's face
grew deadly pale, and she nervously clutched
Nancy's hand.

"Oh! now, after bearing up so well all night,"
said the latter, while her own voice quivered,

" you would not go to break your heart and your child's, too, at the last moment. In pity to her, don't show such signs of grief. What a happy woman I would have been to see my daughter going as Annie is. The morning she left, not one was in the cabin but little Francis— he was little then—who called in on his way to school. And Annie this morning leaves you for a happy land with a thousand blessings on her head."

Soon Annie came out from the room, with her neat black hat and new cloak on, surrounded by a crowd of friends. How pretty she looked, the paleness of her face only serving to reveal more clearly her finely arched, dark eyebrows! Had James O'Rourke seen her at that moment, he would have loved her better than ever, if love could be stronger than his.

Farrell ran from the cottage like one wild ; he could not bear to be present at the parting.

" Now is the time for your fortitude and charity, too, Mrs. Reilly," whispered the old lady, as Annie approached.

" Just kiss your mother and ask her blessing, and leave at once, Annie," said Mrs. Brady. " The less time you spend here now, the better for both of you."

The girl bent over her mother.

"My child! my darling! my own Annie!" exclaimed Mrs. Reilly, "in this, the saddest hour of my life, I call on God to be *just* to that man who drove us apart so soon, and sent you out alone on the world to-day. O Annie! if ever an unhappy mother died of a broken, crushed heart, it will be me if anything befalls you." And mother and daughter were locked in each other's arms. The spectators turned away from the heartrending scene, and a tear came into every eye. "My sweet child, my fond Annie, that was always such a loving daughter to us, it has been a source of sorrow to me since I first watched for your footsteps to think I would one day have to part from you ; but I would have lain cold in my grave long ago had I ever known or thought you would be left a lone bird far away from father, mother, or brother." She sobbed as she pressed the girl close to her heart.

"O mother!" said Annie, "my love for you will be stronger than ever now, and will urge me to make every effort to come to your arms again. Give me your blessing, your fond blessing, and neither of us need fear anything."

"My blessing, and God's choicest blessing, and the blessing of all the saints in heaven for ever be with you, my child," said her mother, raising her hands. "And that blessing I will invoke night and day on your head while God leaves me life."

They held their faces together, mingling their tears in silent, unutterable anguish, till Mrs. Brady said softly in the mother's ear, " Mrs. Reilly, you have blessed your child, we have all blessed her : 'tis needless to delay longer. Your next meeting will be a happy one." And the good woman gently withdrew the arms that embraced the girl, and whispered her to leave at once. After fervently kissing the cold, wet face, Annie ran from the house, and was gone.

It was a beautiful morning in the month of August ; a drop of dew glistened on every blade of grass and on every thorn. The webs of the busy spider covered every tree and shrub, and the lark's first note of welcome to the rising sun was heard from the wood close by.

Farrell joined the group that had followed Annie, and the little crowd set out for the neighboring station ; Maurice had gone on a little before with the trunk, to have it marked, and ready when the train would arrive. Farrell intended accompanying her as far as Queenstown, but Francis was to return from the station to his mother.

The morning had passed away so quickly that, just as they came within view of the station the whistle of the engine sounded shrilly over a hill close by, and the next moment a long line of cars shot out on the plain before them, and swept up to the station. A delay of half an hour, however, would occur, and they reached the platform just as an old priest, with long, white hair and bent figure, was giving his parting blessing to a number of emigrants who knelt on the platform around him. Annie hastily made her way and knelt down on the edge of the crowd. Amongst them were young men and girls, married men and their wives and children. Even grandfathers and grandmothers, who had bravely struggled for a lifetime to live and die in the old land, knelt there to receive the last blessing from an Irish priest, and then face the wild Atlantic, probably to die of hardships by the way, or lay their bones to rest as soon as they reached the new land.

Beneath the face of God, there is no sadder sight than to witness those old, helpless, broken-hearted creatures, who love their native land next to their God, when every earthly hope has failed, gathered at the foot of the saintly priest, to ask his blessing on their flight. What hope they place in this last benediction in the Isle of Saints God only can tell!

A warning whistle announced to Annie and the others that it was time to go aboard. She hastily took farewell of her friends, and having affectionately kissed her brother, and bade him be good and true to their aged parents, and have every hope in her, hurried into the car, followed by her father.

Her brother and friends stood together on the platform, replying to the white handkerchief which kept waving to them from the carriage window till the train moved out of sight.

It was late in the evening when they arrived in Queenstown, and, as the ship by which Annie intended going was not expected in till the following morning, they sought a lodging-house for the night. The lodging-house was within view of the beautiful harbor, and the young girl sat by the window in the dim twilight watching the emigrants clambering on board a vessel which had just arrived from Liverpool. Farrell sat with his elbows resting on a little round table which stood in the middle of the room, eagerly scanning an engraving of New York Bay which hung on the opposite wall.

A strange feeling came over Annie. She could not take her eyes from the ship, and she heartily wished she had been in time to sail by it. Why she felt thus she could not tell. Her memory wandered to James O'Rourke. What sort of ship did he cross over in? How did he spend his time aboard, and what kind of friends did he

make? Did he enliven them with his flute, or
did he stand silently alone looking out on the
wide waters? This latter she thought more
likely.

It grew dark, and, though she could no longer
see those on board, the tall mast and yard-arms were
yet faintly visible through the fading light, and she
could hear the voices of the sailors as they called
out to each other. A light shone on deck. A
man carrying a lantern passed along close by the
bulwark, and the reflection fell on the form of a
man standing alone with his arms folded, just
as Annie thought a moment before James would
stand. She knew the figure. No; it could not
be James. He had gone a week ago. The man
looked down the gangway, and held the light
before him. God! if he would only turn its light
the other way. She leaned from the window,
and strained her eyes almost to bursting. At
length the light turned in the coveted direction,
and she saw the figure move slowly away. It
could be no other. Yes; it was no other than
James O'Rourke. She knew the form, the clothes,
everything. Surely it was he. She had presence of mind enough not to alarm her father,
knowing how useless it would be. She waited
and watched, in hopes to see the light return.
But, no; the sky darkened for rain, and she could no

loi.ger see even the main-mast ; still her eyes were bent in that direction. Soon the rain began to fall. A flash of lightning filled the room, followed by a crash of thunder that shook the very walls. Annie seemed not to notice it. Another flood of lightning, more terrible than the first, filled the air outside, and, darting outwards, revealed the ship slowly moving out to sea.

Neither Annie nor her father slept much during the night, and both were up early and waiting at the ticket-office for the clerk to open. Farrell paid the passage-money, and gave her besides all he could possibly spare, in case she should need it when she reached New York.

About noon, the noble ship came in sight, and soon anchored in the harbor. The parting between her father and Annie was quite as affecting as the morning one. Having her luggage taken aboard, she joined the stream of human cargo scrambling and jostling each other up the ship's side.

CHAPTER XI.

LIVERPOOL MAN-CATCHERS AND LODGING-HOUSES.

E shall now return to James O'Rourke, whom we left in the rather unpleasant position of bidding a hasty good-by to his sweetheart, while he dreaded every moment the faithful upholders of justice and fair play in Ireland would be upon him. After parting from Annie, he turned his steps northward, hoping to reach Dublin before the authorities there could be apprised of his flight. He deemed it better to take this direction, as the police would be certain to warn their brothers at Queenstown to look out for him. Neither did he think it prudent to travel by the main roads, but kept to the by-lanes and open country.

The short night passed quickly away, but, when morning came, James had left his home a long way behind, and found himself in a part of the country totally unknown to him. By making enquiries of some laborers who were going to their toil at that early hour, he found the road to Dublin; and, as his apprehensions had calmed considerably since he left his native county, he struck boldly into the road, and that evening, tired and footsore, reached the city. The Liverpool boat was about to leave in a few minutes after he reached the dock, and, as he did not care to delay in the capital, he took passage, and was soon out on the Irish Sea.

James and his fellow-passengers had a pleasant voyage. The night was calm and fine on their departure, and continued so till morning; when, just as tall wreaths of smoke began to curl up from the houses along the Mersey, they reached Liverpool. A motley crowd of ship-runners and lodging-house keepers met the passengers on their landing, and surrounded them like a pack of hungry wolves; some crying out they represented such a ship—" the very best on the ocean " —and beseeching all sensible passengers who valued their health and future prosperity to take no other; some frantically roaring out the numerous striking qualities of their boarding-house: what attention—we don't doubt that—what good meals, what cleanliness was to be found there. It would be much better for those man-catchers, as they are called, not to mention cleanliness, lest some inquisitive emigrant should look at their faces and hands, and begin to reflect, till, seeing they told one lie, probably doubt all they

had to say. But shout, and yell, and declaim
they will, and always give their voices a little
higher pitch at the word cleanliness. James, not
being encumbered with much baggage, escaped
pretty well till he reached the dock, where he
stood looking at the scramble, and din, and noise
going on on the gangway and around him. It
looked like a fierce charge on a well-fought field,
only more terrible ; for, when a man fell here, no
companion in swind—in arms, bore him to the
rear.

The man-catchers bore down on the passengers as they left the boat, the latter slowly but
steadily driving them back. Old scoundrels, who
had made emigrant-swindling a lifelong business,
and were very much attached to it now, were
knocked down and walked over every day by
their stronger competitors ; but, nothing daunted,
they would be at their post the following morning as determined as ever.

At length, when the strife subsided, and the as-
sailants began to carry off their spoils, in the shape
of innocent men, women, and children who had
probably never seen a city before, James, seeing
a man standing with his back towards him, clad
in very shiny black, looking out on the river,
made up his mind to ask him the way to the
ticket-office. Thinking he must be some distin-

guished personage, James approached respect-
fully, and said, "Please, sir, will you be kind
enough to direct me to the shipping-office? I
am going to America."

The man turned towards him, and, if James
O'Rourke had been a keen observer, he would
have seen at once that a front view of the gentleman was hardly in keeping with the appearance
he presented from behind. His face was very
long and irregular, his mouth very wide—much
wider than nature had intended it should be, as
a deep, bluish scar on one side added considerably to its proportions. His eyes were very small
and round, and seemed determined, through time,
on making their way through his brain to the
other side. His nose seemed to have met the
same adverse fate as his mouth. It hung down
in a heavy red bunch in front, owing, we think,
to the part nearest the eyes being completely
flattened, probably by some blunt instrument, as
the doctors say. His forehead—well, that very
important part of his head was concealed from
view by an immense wide-brimmed hat, which
had once been as shiny as his coat, but was now
assuming an auburn hue. He wore his coat
buttoned up close, a yellowish necktie, but no
collar.

"My dear young fellow, hi shall be 'appy to

direct you," said he, turning to James, on hearing his question. " Step this 'ere way a little." And he led him a few yards further away from the boat. " Hof course, you want to sail by the best line?"

"Certainly I do, sir," said James, after a little hesitation, "if it does not cost any more; for, to tell you the truth—"

" Not ha penny more than the leakiest hold tub as crosses the Atlantic. 'Ere his the name hof the ship; she sails to-morrow morning."

" Thank God !" thought James, delighted at the prospect of spending so little time in Liverpool.

Now, it so happened that the gentleman, in showing the notice to James, flaunted it a little too much, so that it caught the eyes of a number of disappointed man-catchers, who were standing here and there, looking very rapacious and sullen. In a moment they were upon them, pushing bills into James's hand, and each begging of him to put no trust in the others, but be guided by him. The old gentleman was pushed to the outside of the crowd in a moment, but his frantic warnings could be heard above all. One in his desperation caught him by the hand, and tried to pull it open, that he might leave his card there.

" Let me speak, for heaven's sake," said James.

"Yes, sir; yes, sir; say whatever you have to say, and come on with me," exclaimed half a dozen voices.

"I am going with none of you, blast you!" shouted James, dashing from their midst. "This gentleman," pointing to the man he had first spoken to, "has kindly consented to do all I want for me."

"All right, go with him; I wish you luck. You'll not get skinned. Oh! no," said the same voices.

"What do they mean by attacking a person in that way?" asked James of the other, who had taken his arm to lead him off.

"Ho! that's the way as they do things haround 'ere hin general," replied the other, pulling down his tie, which in the scuffle had got up around his ears. "You're ha fort'nate man to miss 'em."

"Please direct me to the office," said James, looking back at the crowd. "I'll leave Liverpool as soon as I can."

"Ho! you must not judge Liverpool by what you see 'ere this mornin'," said his companion. "When you see the place as I'll take ye to, your hopinion of the Hinglish 'ill change; but we'll go to the hoffice first."

They walked a long way along the docks, his companion still holding James by the arm, and

pointing out all the places of interest to stran-
gers—which, by the way, were chiefly high, old,
dirty-looking stores, with broken doors and
windows, outside of which sat groups of ill-
clad, ill-favored looking men, black with smoke
and grease ; and an occasional large dray, pulled
by huge, lazy horses—so lazy that you would want
to be close by before knowing whether they were
moving or not—was also an object of curiosity to
James. At length they turned up a side street,
walking over heaps of half-naked women and children at every step, till they reached a somewhat
neat-looking building—neat only when contrasted
with its neighbors—and entered an office on the
ground floor. The only furniture of any kind it
contained was a triangular desk of very doubtful
material, and a fat, dull-eyed, middle-aged man
of undoubted Saxon nationality. He was eating
a lump of cheese, which he held in the palm of
his hand, and did not seem to notice them as they
entered.

"The best-'arted man in the world," whispered the guide.

James thought, if that were so, it had very little
control over his manner; but he said nothing.

"How d'ye do, Mr. Bluffy ?" said the other, approaching the desk. "I 'opes as yer well, sir."

"Well enough," was the reply. "Have you

done anything to-day ? I am afraid you're going in the back of the books here, Lantern."

" Why, 'ow is that, Mr. Bluffy?" said that gentleman, with a rueful look, which was his best look. " Han't hi hout hearly and late a watchin' and a strivin' for this 'ere company ? "

" That may all be," said Bluffy, reaching for a pint of ale which a boy had just entered with, " but you an't doing anything."

Mr. Bluffy put the measure to his mouth and drained it to the last drop, smacked his lips, handed it back to the boy, and added : " There's where the mistake comes in."

" Do you call this 'ere nothin' ? " said Mr. Lantern, pointing to James. " Hi took 'im from thirty on 'em ; hi did that, Mr. Bluffy."

" Well, well," said the other, " a bob, and no more about it."

" Ho Mr. Bluffy, Mr. Bluffy !" And he put an old, torn red handkerchief, which came out of his pocket like a rope, to his eyes. " Hi earns it 'ard as hany man, hand why not "—a sob—" give me the same has hanother man ? "

" You know the rules," said the other : " one bob for one, three bob for two, and so forth."

" Them 'ere rules is 'ard on a poor man," blubbered Lantern.

But looking towards James, and noticing

he was not so shabbily clad as the majority
of emigrants, he brightened up a little, and
approaching near to his patron, whispered a
word in his ear. The latter let his heavy eyes
fall on James, and said :

"All right, if it can be done."

"Come 'ere now, my young friend," said Lantern, "hand get yer ticket."

James walked up to the desk.

"Give me the money," said the man behind it.

"How much is it, sir?" asked James anxiously.

"£5 15s." was the reply.

O'Rourke's face flushed a little. "I thought,
sir," he said, "£5 10s. was the highest rate of
passage?"

Bluffy looked at Lantern, and the latter quickly
said :

"The hextra vive bob his for hextra accommodation. Mr. Bluffy, the best-'arted man in
Hingland, says as 'ow you'll not be treated like
hanother passenger."

"Oh! but I am satisfied to rough it with the
rest," said James. "My funds are very low."

"All right," grunted Bluffy, "if you want to
sleep up by the engine, and have the smoke and
dirt blowing over you every night." And he began to make out the ticket.

"Young man, you're ha destroyin' of yourself. You may get blinded," whispered Lantern, clutching James by the arm. "Let me hadvise you, has a honest man as does fair by 'is fellow-man, to change your mind."

"I'll pay it, then," said James; "but it seems strange to charge more than the advertised rate."

"Your wisdom 'ill make yer fortin', young man," said Lantern, not heeding the latter part of the other's remark.

James paid the money, and turned away; but, as he did so, the corner of his eye caught Mr. Lantern picking up two of the very half-crowns he had paid, and thrusting them hurriedly into his pocket. He was about to make some remark, but, thinking it might be some money due him by the other, he merely sighed and wished himself out of Liverpool.

Mr. Lantern joined him outside the office, and conducted him down to the docks again. and along in the direction from which they had just come, then up a very narrow, dirty street, with high, bare, miserable-looking houses on each side, which had not received a brush of whitewash or paint in half a century, if they ever received one. The greater part of these buildings were eating and lodging-houses, and the smell of bad meat, rotten cabbage, and garbage of every kind

which they sent into the street made the atmo-
sphere well-nigh intolerable.   At length Mr. Lantern stopped at one of the most ill-looking places
they had met, with an old weather-beaten sign
over the door, on which was scrawled, in almost
unintelligible letters, " Lodging and Entertain-
ment."

" This is the 'ouse where you'll be comfortable
till mornin'," said Lantern.   " Come halong, sir."

James followed him, and, as he entered the
door, the abominable smell that filled the place
was ten times worse than that in the street.   A
small door just inside the entrance opened in a
very dark little room which fronted on the street.
This room, like its brothers in every house in
that street, had its window continually closed
with half-rotten, whitish shutters ; and as these
managed to keep together, the room was
left all day, at any rate, without a single ray
of light.   Its door was standing ajar as James
passed, and, happening to look that way, the
thick darkness, with here and there the back
of an old white chair dimly visible, like a shy
ghost, made him hurry after his guide into the
room directly behind this one.   This latter was
the principal apartment of the establishment.
Though small in size, it served as kitchen, dining-room, laundry, smoking-room, gambling-room,

and, in short, every purpose for which any room could be used.

The only persons within when they entered were an old, very ugly woman, with a large, full, iron-gray face studded over with numerous small projections, out of which grew several long hairs corresponding in color with her face, and a young, fat, sullen-looking girl, who sat so close to the fire that her face shone again. The former sat in the window-sill, peeling potatoes with the blade of an old razor set in a piece of wood, and, as she finished a potato, she threw the skins through a broken pane into—God knows where—outside. The other, who looked decidedly lazy, now and then took hold of a long stick, black from grease and dirt, which stood in a large pot of soup on the fire, and stirred it round and round.

The old lady's face we do not think could assume a cheerful expression on any occasion; so that there may not be much in saying she frowned as Mr. Lantern went over to her. But it was such a wicked, scornful frown, and her eyes flashed so, surely he must be no favorite of hers.

"'E wants to lodge 'ere to-night, Mrs. Vitles. Hi brought 'im 'ere."

Mrs. Witles turned her head from side to side a few times, and resumed her work without making any reply. Mr. Lantern looked around, and the top of his nose grew redder as he saw that James noticed his reception. He turned to Mrs. Witles again, and stood with his knees together, not venturing to say a word.

" Vell," said she at length, throwing down the knife, but without raising her eyes. " Vell."

" Hi brought a lodger to yer, Mrs. Vitles," said Lantern feebly.

" Vell, you know 'e can stay. Vere's yer use in tellin' me? Do yer see any sign on 'im runnin' away?"

" Hi—yer know the reason I tell ye, Mrs. Vitles," said he, with a mean leer, and backing further away.

" Wery well I do," said she, in a loud voice; " but do ye expect me to pay ye afore I knows 'ow much I'm a goin' to make meself?"

Lantern cast a wistful look at the soup, which Mrs. Witles at once interpreted; for she exclaimed:

" Hi'll be blowed if I do. Leave 'ere, now." And she snatched the stick from the soup-pot. " Go, now," continued she, advancing threateningly upon him. " You're more 'arm than good to any place as lets you in on 'em. Make tracks, now."

And as the worthy gentleman backed into the hall, she slammed the door so quickly that it was a miracle his nose escaped.

James sat for a time, oppressed by the heat and smell of the place, and by his own troubled mind ; for, now that he was alone—we may say so, for neither of the women addressed a word to him or even looked towards him—the unhappy state of his father at home, and sorrow and anxiety after Annie, crowded on his mind. So much did these thoughts weigh upon him that he forgot his own unhappy circumstances and uncertain future, and even where he was, till the noise of heavy footsteps outside in the hall roused him. The door was burst open, and a motley crowd of coal-heavers, sailors, old pensioners, browned with the sun of India, thimble-riggers, trick-o'-the-loop men, ballad-singers, and, in short, a sample of all the lower grades of the city crowded into the room.

James looked up and saw dinner was already on the table, and Mrs. Witles busily engaged filling a row of wooden bowls with soup, cabbage, potatoes, and loathsome-looking lumps of fat which the young woman was lifting from the bottom of the pot with her fingers.

The men, such of them as could, climbed over the high form which surrounded the table, and, resting their elbows thereon, began to eat like wolves. Many of the old soldiers and sailors, who were disabled so badly in upholding the majesty

of England that any future attempt of theirs at
stepping over a form must be hopeless, sat down
with their backs to the table, and such of them as
had two hands held the bowl in one of them;
but others, who were not blessed with that number, held it between their knees; and a few who,
happened to want hands and knees both, sat down
on the floor and ate like animals.

James looked on in amazement at the hideous
sight, and made no attempt to join them, till Mrs.
Wittles, when the meal was almost over and some
·of the guests straggling out, said, looking sharply
at him:

"Fall hin, young man, or you'll be too late."

"With your leave, madam," replied he, "I
would rather wait a little."

The poor fellow could no more eat with such a
party than he could fly.

"Hi wouldn't keep my table set hafter the reg-
'lar hour for the queen 'erself, if she was 'ere,"
said Mrs. Witles, snatching a lump of meat from
before a lean old pensioner, which the latter had
stolen from the pot while her back was turned.

James moved over to the table, and, the bowl
being set before him, covered his eyes with his
hands to shut out the sight of a sailor opposite,
who was licking the inside of his bowl like a
dog. Mrs. Witles's plan for the dinner-hour was a

very good one for herself. As soon as she saw a
boarder had his bowl emptied, she immediately
ordered him, with a shake of the soup-stick, to
leave, thereby preventing the possibility of giving
him a second round. This, too, helped James to
get rid of the disgusting fellow across the table
much sooner than otherwise might have happened : for Mrs. Witles's quick eye alighting on
him, she ordered him, with sundry choice epithets,
to go before he'd " eat the bowl."

James tasted a little of the soup, but nothing else. He went into the street, and wandered down as far as the docks again, taking a mental note of everything of remark
he passed, that he might not lose his way coming back. He sat down on the edge of the
quay, and watched the men loading and unload-
ing the ships, and saw several going out to sea,
some for China and Japan and other far distant
places. A number of vessels, too, arrived during
the evening, and, as he saw the passengers coming
ashore, wondered what kind of country they came
from, what sort of cities and people did it contain, or were they as dirty as Liverpool.

He remained there till it began to grow dark
and a few of the lamps around him were lighted,
when he turned and walked back to the lodging-
house.

If the streets presented a wretched appearance in daytime, they looked doubly so at night. They were literally filled with poverty and vice of the very worst kind. Beggars with awful-looking sores stood or lay in knots around the lamp-posts, frantically telling the wretched passers-by of their sufferings and pain. A blind or disabled musician of some kind, clad in rags, scraped or thumbed a miserable instrument before nearly every door. Drunken men and women rushed into the streets with yells, curses, and shouts of obscenity, occasionally stopping for a moment to dance to the wretched music, then hurrying on, trampling over the children and helpless.

Bad as his lodging-house was within, it was some relief to James to escape from such a scene. None of the other boarders had returned, and he requested to be shown to his bed. Mrs. Witles handed him a candle, and, pointing up the dingy old stairs, told him to push open the door of the first room he met, and lie down on any bed he chose. Of beds he had a noble choice. The room, which, by the way, was the entire floor, was so closely packed with beds that no one might attempt to walk from one side of the apartment to the other, except he stepped from bed to bed. James held the candle down between

two beds, that he might see the floor; this was
no easy task either, for it was covered to the
depth of a couple of inches with dust and other
dirt, all of which did not belong to the inanimate
kingdom. He raised the candle and looked
around the room, on the green and black walls,
down which the rain had poured for years and
years; and from the quantity of cobwebs which
covered the ceiling—what of it remained—and
the angles of the room, it was evident Mrs. Witles made very little use of her broom.

James, being very much exhausted from hardship and long want of sleep, selected a bed on
the outer row, which looked as if it had not been
occupied for some time, lay down on its edge,
and soon fell asleep. How long he slept he knew
not, till he was aroused by the noise of voices
around him—loud, coarse voices—and, looking
up, saw the same group he had met at dinner; some walking over the beds to reach their
own on the far side, others crowding in at the
door, and one and all in an advanced stage of in-
toxication.

Some were pale, sick, and sad; others were
sentimental, who wept to themselves over past
attachments in their own and other lands; a few
were belligerent, and, assuming numerous fighting attitudes, boasted they were afraid of no man

in " Hingland, without reference to the present
company"; and the old soldier from whom Mrs.
Witles snatched the lump of fat stood up on his
bed, and screamed in a dismal, broken voice a
verse of " Rule, Britannia !"   By-and-by, all fell
here and there on the beds, in different positions,
and went to sleep.   But so stifling was the atmo-
sphere from the fumes of bad whisky that James
went out on the landing, where he remained till
daylight.

As soon as Mrs. Witles appeared, he paid her
the amount of his bill, and went down to the
docks to wait till the time for going aboard would
arrive.   Soon other emigrants, with packages and
bundles of all kinds, began to assemble at the
quay, and James went amongst such of them as
he knew were from Ireland, and talked with them
till the hour for starting came.

About mid-day, the ship weighed anchor, and
steamed down the Mersey.   James O'Rourke was
not much of a philosopher ; but, as he stood on
deck, looking at the noble buildings which rose
here and there on the Cheshire coast, and thought
of what he had witnessed in Liverpool, he could
not help thinking that a nation composed of two
such extremes must one day break in the centre.

The passage down the Irish Sea was beautiful.
James waited with great anxiety for their arrival

at Queenstown, that he might, probably for the last time, feast his eyes on the hills and valleys of his native land. But to his great mortification, it was almost dark night when they entered the harbor. The day, even at sea, had been very warm, and with evening came lowering clouds and other signs of a storm. For a time, he stood on deck looking at the row of lights along the harbor, thinking of home and the base villany that had driven him thence; of Annie—what was she doing now? This was about the time they used to meet on the river's bank. Did she go there alone now, and sit and think of him, and remember him in her prayers, as she had promised to do? Was it beyond hope that they would ever meet again?

This thought sickened his heart so much that he leaned against the cabin-door, and turned his eyes away from the coast. A gruff officer, carrying a light, passed down the deck, and ordered him "to stand some place else." He went down to his berth, and, throwing himself on his face, wept til the ship was far out to sea.

CHAPTER XII.

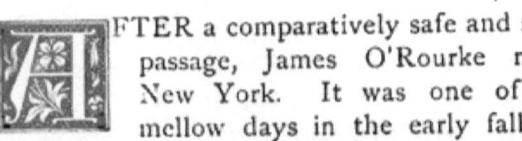FTER a comparatively safe and speedy passage, James O'Rourke reached New York. It was one of those mellow days in the early fall when everything looks so serene and calm that the anxious passengers were landed. How beautiful New York Harbor looked! The waters seemed asleep on the bosom of the bay, save where disturbed by the lively ferry-boats ploughing their way backwards and forwards in every direction, and the little snorting tugs, puffing in and out here and there, busy as bees of a June morning. A number of large, majestic-looking ships, that had just come in from all ports of the world, lay out in the stream, looking weary after their long voyage.

It being early day, the passengers were not delayed at Castle Garden overnight, except such as chose to wait for friends who were expecting them. James had no friends, and he walked into the streets and up along Broadway, wondering at the size, and beauty, and cheerful look of the buildings along that noble thoroughfare. It was at the time of day when Broadway is at its liveliest, lined with wagons, carriages, carts, and drays, and the sidewalk so crowded with people hurrying along that it is impossible for any of them to make much speed. James walked on— he knew not where—looking on himself as the most lonely and friendless of the great throng. At length he came to what seemed to him a neglected waste of ground, which, having mortally offended the city in some way, was left behind, forgotten, haggard, and cheerless. Near the centre of this waste stood a large building in a half-finished state, looking so dreary that the ill fate of the neighborhood seemed to have visited it at last.

A number of men were standing around the doors or sitting on the steps of the building, and all looking so much like men that had nothing to do, that James thought it might not inconvenience any of them much to tell him where he might find work. So approaching a gentleman with a wide-leafed straw hat, a tight-fitting coat, much too short for him, and very long, wide pantaloons, who stood on the end of a row picking his teeth, James asked :

"Please, sir, can you tell me where I may find employment? I am a stranger here."

"Most undoubtedly, sir; follow me," said the gentleman, putting his tooth-pick in his vest pocket. "Come along, sir."

James, delighted beyond measure at this sudden good luck, hurried after his new friend, but found it no very easy task to keep up with him. He had such a happy method of diving past crowds which jostled against the other that he had once or twice to wait for him on the corner. At length the gentleman swept into a low, narrow door in one of the side streets, and when James rushed in after him, he found him seated behind a neat little desk, looking as composed as if he had been sitting there since morning.

"So you want employment, do you?" said he, surveying James from head to foot.

"Yes, sir," replied the latter.

"What kind do you prefer?" said he, opening a book which lay on the desk before him. "We have a variety."

"Well, sir," replied James with a smile, "I am not afraid of any kind of work, but would of course prefer whichever pays best.'

"Let me see," said the other, closing his eyes and resting his chin on his hand, "let me see. You are strong enough to work in a dry-goods store?"

"You mean, sir—"

"I mean what you call a cloth-shop in the Old Country."

"Oh! yes; I beg your pardon, sir," said James. greatly elated. "Certainly I am, sir."

"You landed this morning, eh?" said the gentleman.

"This morning, sir?"

"Any friends in New York?"

"No, sir."

"All alone, eh?"

"Quite so, sir."

"Well, now, sir, I'll tell you what I'll do. You give me three dollars, and I'll send you right up to the establishment."

James felt greatly surprised at this, for he really thought the gentleman was an extensive employer himself. He had never heard of an "intelligence office," and was quite at a loss what to think. He couldn't be a swindler, having such a handsome place.

"No; he *must* be an employer, and probably wants this money as security for a day or two, till he sees how I get on," thought James.

And looking at the gentleman again, and seeing him busy writing. and apparently utterly oblivious of his presence, was confirmed in this latter idea.

" I'll pay the money, sir," said he, taking from his pocket a few shillings and one half-crown, which was his entire store.

The gentleman thought it most remarkable, but nevertheless it was true, that the coins when changed into dollars amounted to just the required number and ten cents over.   So he swept it into a drawer, and, throwing a ten-cent stamp on the desk, drew a piece of paper to him, and, having written a few words on it with violet ink, handed it to James.   The latter glanced at it and said :

" What way am I to go there, sir ?"

"You see I am so busy, or I would take you up myself.   But, anyway, all you have to do is to cross over five blocks to your right, then down a long street you'll see with a marble building on the up-town corner, then one block to your right, then take the cars—you know the street-cars— and ride eleven blocks more, and any one can point out Van Sleuthers & Duckey's dry-goods store to you.   Go inside, and show them that address, and you're all right."

James thanked him, left the office, and went in search of Van Sleuthers & Duckey's.

That he did not find it, and that there was no such firm in the city, it is needless to say.   He had been swindled out of the last penny by an "intelligence agent"; and after travelling up and down the streets, looking at every sign, stopping to make enquiries at every clothing establishment, he found himself at nightfall close by the East River, footsore, weary, and dejected. He sat down on a log on one of the docks, and, covering his eyes with his hands, began to think over his forlorn, desolate state.

In a large city, without a friend, without one face he had ever known, without a single penny in his pocket. Where to spend the night or get a morsel to eat he knew not; he had spent the ten cents riding up and down in search of Van Sleuthers & Duckey's. He sat a prey to these thoughts for some time, till, raising his head, he saw coming leisurely towards him, from the direction of the street, a man in his shirt-sleeves, smoking a large briar-wood pipe.

As he approached, James could see he was of his own race, and made up his mind to speak to him. This was no difficult matter, for the stranger came on, puffing like an engine, and, sitting down beside him, remarked it was a fine night.

O'Rourke saw at once, from his large, rough hands, that he belonged to the working-class, and, observing his neat white shirt and black tie, and everything he wore so clean, thought of the miserable appearance of the English working-men.

"You're not long out from the ould counthry, I think," said he kindly.

"No, indeed," said James. "I came ashore this morning."

"Well, well," said the man, moving close to him, "I am glad to see any one so late from the ould dart. How is things there now; anything better?"

"Oh! much the same as usual," replied James. "Improvements come very slowly in Ireland."

"That's so, that's so, me friend," said the other, with a sigh. "But the people an't starving as they wor when I left there?"

"Not so bad as that now," said James.

"Do you live around here?" asked the stranger, after a pause.

"I have no home," said James, drawing back his head a little.

"No home," said the other, "and a greenhorn; why, that's rough. I suppose be that ye mane you haven't got any money neither."

"Not a penny," was the reply.

Then James told him how he had been cheated by the intelligence agent.

"You're not the first who has been fleeced by thim robbers," said the other in a rage. "They swindle dozens of poor innocent people every day, and you'll niver hear of one of thim bein' arristed. But," added he, checking himself, "it can't be helped now, and I'll niver see one of my countrymen that desarves it out in the streets at night while I have a room; so you must come wid me to-night. The ould woman 'ill find some place for you to sleep."

James thanked him again and again, and, after enjoying a smoke from his pipe, they walked up the dock and along the street a little way, till they came to a somewhat neat-looking brick house with a wooden stoop. The man entered, and both went up a flight of very clean but carpetless stairs to the third story, and, turning the knob of the door, entered a tidily furnished room of comfortable dimensions. Over the wooden mantel-piece hung a handsome engraving of Archbishop Hughes, side by side with another of St. Patrick, and on the opposite wall hung a picture of Killarney Lakes. Several other pictures, some of Irish clergy, some of American, were fastened round the walls, all very tastefully arranged.

There was no person in the room on their entrance, and the man, seeing James look closely at the archbishop's likeness, began to tell numerous stories of his kindness and benevolence. After some time, a woman came in, carrying a basket on her arm; and from the appearance of her face, and the trim, cleanly way in which she was clad, James knew at once whose taste had arranged the room.

"Well, well, Terence, and what a man you are," said she, laying down the basket, and looking at her husband with a smile, "to leave housekeeping."

"Oh! in troth, I was afraid she'd begin to screech whin ye'd be gone, Bridget, so I left her inside with Mrs. Kearney. She stays as quiet wid her as wid yourself," said her husband.

"Oh! just so; anything to get rid of the job. But keep quiet now; she's asleep in Mrs. Kearney's arms, and I'll bring her in and put her in the cradle."

The woman left the room, and soon returned, carrying in her arms a little babe of a few months old, and, shaking her hand at her husband to say nothing, lest he should rouse the infant, went through the passage-way into another room.

The man conversed with James for awhile, then, telling him he'd be back in a moment, followed his wife. Both soon returned, and James could see from the kind, sympathetic look the woman gave him that her husband had been telling his story.

"Excuse me," said the man, "but ye haven't tould me yer name."

James told him.

"In troth, and a good name it is. My own is Terence McManus, and this is Mrs. McManus, and that sleepy youngster ye seen a minute ago is Mary McManus. So we know each other all roun' now, and are quite at our aise."

The agreeable, honest, good-natured manner of the man did make James feel much easier in mind than he had felt for some time. Mrs. McManus prepared a good meal, of which all three partook. This over, they sat together, and talked over matters in the old and new country. One important point to James came out from this conversation, and that was he learned that his host, who worked along the docks, being what is commonly called a 'longshoreman, would find him employment at the same business the following day.

CHAPTER XIII.

ANNIE'S VOYAGE.—HOW EMIGRANTS ARI
TREATED ON SHIPBOARD.

URING the first three days out, Annie
was very sea-sick, and unable to come
on deck. So much did she suffer from
this distressing illness and her own
grief of mind that she hardly cared whether the
ship sank or not. At times during these days,
she thought she would surely have died were it
not for the kindness and attention shown her by
a young woman from Dublin, who was going out
to meet her husband in the West. Though
greatly burdened with her little son, who continued ill all the way, she spent every moment
she could with Annie, getting up at least a dozen
times during the night to see how she felt; often
going to the doctor to tell him of her state, and
beg him to send her some relief, and almost as
often getting rudely repulsed.

Of all the sinecures on land or sea, that of ship
doctor, as far as the poor steerage passengers are
concerned, is the most idle. A ship doctor is
generally a very stylish gentleman—a snob—who

knows far more about the fashions than about medicine, and thinks all that is required of him is to strut the deck, and laugh and chat with the cabin passengers. Those in the steerage are so much beneath his notice that nothing can induce him to go below, even if a life depended on the very act. He may, if caught in the *humor*, condescend to order a poor sufferer some medicine on the report of the steward—a gentleman generally as ignorant in cases of sickness as himself.

What drug the model M.D. on this occasion sent Annie she would not venture to touch, and this probably accounted for her being able to go on deck the following morning in company with her kind friend.

It was a beautiful morning at sea. The sun shone bright and soft on the waste of calm water, and the ship was making rapid headway. Annie and her friend, Mrs. Duffy, sat down on deck close by the bulwark. The deck was literally swarming with men, women, and children from every country in Europe, every nationality keeping in little groups by themselves. Englishmen, with long side-whiskers, short coats, and moist eyes, stood or lay together in knots, sometimes silent and sad, and occasionally talking in low murmuring accents; Irishmen, stout, hearty, and pleasant, smoked, chatted, laughed together and seemed to take more notice of what was going on around them than any other people; Germans, black and greasy, lay in heaps together, men and women, and seemed to occupy their whole time eating. All the other passengers, especially the Irish, disliked them; their hands and faces were so dirty, and their old rags smelled so disgustingly, that we pity any company in a close room who would have a German amongst them. A few garrulous and excitable Frenchmen walked up and down on one side of the deck, talking loudly; Italian organ-grinders and beggars had their place, and two or three swarthy Spaniards leaned over the bulwark, looking down at the water.

At a little distance from and directly in front of Annie and her friend sat a Scotchman alone by himself. Not that he was by any means the only Scotchman on board, but he seemed to be of a sentimental turn of mind, and probably loved solitude. He had a very long face and forehead, whitish-colored hair, a very red beard, and wore a short frock-coat of heavy, coarse material, with a row of immense buttons on each side, short, tight trowsers, and, when he chose to wear it, a torn glazed cap. One arm rested on a coil of rope behind him, in the hand of which he held a large-sized snuff-box, and the other hand

was employed in occasionally carrying the snuff
to his nose. Whether he was an old man with a
white head, or a very young man with false
whiskers, or a middle-aged one, it would take
some person well skilled in those matters to say.
From the time Annie and her friend came on
deck, he had not taken his eyes off the former;
and turn her head in what direction she would to
avoid his gaze, he moved so as to watch her face.
Whether it was from admiration, or curiosity, or
impertinence, his countenance gave no indication.
Annie felt greatly annoyed, and, not wishing to
go below in the damp smell, and seeing no place
on deck to escape to, mentioned the matter to
her friend.

"Oh! I have noticed him," said Mrs. Duffy,
laughing. "He is some stupid lout; don't let
him annoy you."

Annie laughed at this remark, and they chatted
away lively and soon forgot him; but never for a
second did he change his look.

At length a number of those on deck went
below, and the two friends rose and went to
another place behind the engine, where they
found a more comfortable seat. They had hardly
seated themselves, when the Scotchman came
and lay down, this time on the deck, about the
same distance from them, and turned his eyes on

Annie again. She was so much alarmed that she begged of the other to come below at once.

"Oh! nonsense," was the reply, " are we going down there because of that awkward fellow? Leave him to me, and, if he attempts to speak to you, I'll insult him so badly that, if he was as stupid again, he'll annoy you no more."

Annie in her heart thanked Providence she had such a friend. If she were alone, what would she do? He would frighten her to death.

At length the dinner-hour arrived, and, as they were about to descend the ladder, Annie felt a light tap on her shoulder, and, looking up, her eyes met her tormentor's dull gaze. She clutched her friend's arm, but, before the latter could speak, he was gone in amongst the crowd clambering down to the table.

Annie's heart throbbed so, and she felt so very much annoyed, that she could not eat any of the choice morsels which her friend took from a little basket in her trunk. It was a hard task to induce her to go on deck that evening, but Mrs. Duffy begged of her so much for her health's sake not to remain in that " hole," as she called it, and promised so fervently to put an end to the Scotchman's annoyance in case he should renew it, that at length she consented to go up again.

They climbed up on the forward deck, the mother taking her little boy, who felt somewhat better, and sat watching the water-fowls flying about and dipping down to the water here and there; wondering where those birds built their nests, or were there any islands near.

Annie had not quite recovered from the shock she had received, and was yet very restless, turning her head in the direction of the ladder now and then, and starting at every glazed cap she saw appearing. Mrs. Duffy drew her closer to her side, and, putting her arm around her waist, told her she had nothing to dread. At length both, happening to look round, saw the ungainly figure of the Scotchman looming into view up the ladder.

"Heavens! there he is again," exclaimed Annie, clinging to her friend. "He'll frighten me to death."

Mrs. Duffy fixed her eyes steadily upon him as he lumbered up the deck. When he came within a few yards of them, he hesitated, stopped, came a little nearer, pulled out his snuff-box, and, coming up to them, held it open towards Annie, without saying a word.

"We don't want your snuff, thank you," said Mrs. Duffy, shaking her head with a frown.

"I ony want to gie this lassie a pinch," said

he, thrusting the box into Annie's face. **The** poor girl was pale with terror.

"You begone, sir!" exclaimed her friend, jump ing to her feet, "and annoy this young girl no more with look or word of yours, or I'll com- plain to the captain. She is young, and not long from home, and not used to looking at such frights as you."

"Ah wull—" he began, moving backwards a step.

"Say no more. Leave here, now, or I'll go to the captain directly." And she moved as if to fulfil the threat, when he turned and shambled away down the length of the deck, down the lad- der, and, when he had about time to reach there, they saw him standing very demure-looking, with his back against the bulwark.

Mrs. Duffy laughed so heartily when he was gone at his awkward look and manner that Annie could not help joining her, and they laughed together till the tears rolled down their cheeks. The Scotchman annoyed them no further during the voyage.

Any time he chanced to see them, he might venture to steal a look at Annie; but, if Mrs. Duffy happened to catch him, he quickly made his way out of sight. Nothing further worthy of notice occurred to our heroine during the voyage, which may be termed a pleasant one, excepting a few stormy days crossing the banks of New-foundland, when the face of the ocean changed from its calm aspect, the waves ran high and angry, tossing the ship from side to side, drifting tin cans, kettles, boxes, passengers, and baskets hither and thither in every direction. The storm lulled as they approached the American coast, and on a beautiful warm evening Sandy Hook lightship came in view. All crowded to the vessel's side, crushing and climbing over each other, to get a view of the new land in which they intended living.

What a moment it. is for those kept down with poverty and oppression at home, toiling in hunger and exposure to enrich the very ones to whom they owe their degradation, when their weary eyes first rest on America's shore! Once there, they know tyranny can claim them no more, and that every advantage, every justice allowed an honest people on earth, will be their share.

When the ship had sailed up the bay and cast anchor, it was nightfall, and the passengers learn-ed they could not go ashore till morning. What an anxious, busy night it was on board: every one putting in the best order they could what little they possessed, that they might make as good an appearance as possible when they reached New York. Packing up, bundling up, tying up, loosing and unloosing, washing and shaving, were going on in every quarter below ; while those who had none of these things to do lined the ship's side, watching the lights along the river and in the city, till the steward announced all would have to go to bed till morning. Little use in sending them there ; for not one passenger on board could sleep that night.

Mrs. Duffy, who did not intend staying any length of time in New York, but to hurry on to her husband in Ohio, however promised to remain with Annie till she saw her on the right way to Kitty Brady.

Poor Annie felt very sad and timid. A thousand disturbing thoughts came into her mind. What if Kitty had left New York, and was not to be found, and that she should be left alone in the streets of the large city ? And even if Kitty was where she still expected her, she might lose her way, and probably meet the Scotchman or somebody like him.

These and numerous other apprehensions she mentioned to Mrs. Duffy, who only laughed at some, and chided her good-naturedly for others.

Both were up at break of day, and sat, and walked, and watched till the tender came out to take the passengers ashore. What a rush was there then! Heaps of trunks and other baggage, piled in every shape, covered the deck; men and women rushed frantically around to discover their own, and the noise and confusion of tongues must have resembled very much that which put an end to the tower of Babel. At length, passengers and baggage arrived at Castle Garden.

CHAPTER XIV.

ANNIE AT CASTLE GARDEN.—HOW PASSENGERS ARE TREATED THERE.

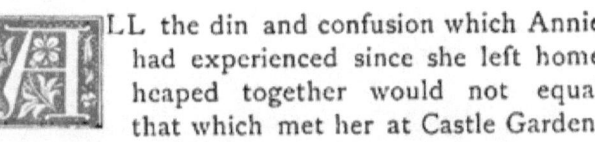LL the din and confusion which Annie had experienced since she left home heaped together would not equal that which met her at Castle Garden. When the tenders reached the dock, the passengers made a mad rush for the shore, crowding over each other up the gangway. The trunks and baggage were landed in the most confused manner. A person would imagine it was the first obligation those employed for that purpose owed to the emigrants, to break and smash their articles as much as possible. It seemed to be the rule to throw all the small and frail boxes ashore first, and then fling the heavier and stronger ones on top of them. Locks were knocked off, lids and sides broken in, and the contents of several strewn like a wreck along the dock. The passengers tried frantically to save their property, and, in doing so, had to contend with the vulgar abuse and often blows of the officials. Some old and feeble men and women, and young girls, saw

all they possessed in the world trampled under
the feet of the excited crowd; and, helpless to
prevent the injury, turned away and began to
cry. It was only the strong and rugged could save
their share in such a place, and that only after
desperate exertions.

A person looking on at one of these scenes
could not help thinking that any strong enough
to carry away their effects from such a place were
able to get along in America as far as muscle was
concerned.

Annie's trunk, being made of strong oak, received no further injury than being thrown bottom upwards on a number of small paper ones;
so all she had to do was to wait till the confusion
would abate, to have it taken inside.

That which contained Mrs. Duffy's articles did
not escape so fortunately. She found it, after a
laborious search, broken open, and a quantity of
linen she was taking to her husband gone. The
poor woman wrung her hands, and ran here and
there relating her misfortune to and asking advice
of every man whom she saw looked like an official.
Not one of them even made her a reply. So all
she could do was to wring her hands again, and
gather up what was left behind in a corner of her
shawl, for the trunk was a total wreck.

Annie rendered her good benefactress all the

assistance in her power, and Mrs. Duffy, being of
such a cheerful disposition, was soon laughing at
the figure she cut with the bundle in her shawl.

A thick-set, rough, decidedly bad-looking man,
seeing Annie standing by her trunk, hurried over
and asked her if she wished it taken inside.

Annie was about to say yes, when her companion hastily interposed, and said, " No, not
yet."

The fellow, seeing he would have got the
" job," as he called it, were it not for her, heaped
a volley of foul abuse on the poor woman, and
even shook his fist in her face, to the great amusement of two officials who were standing by smoking very long cigars.

At length, when the greater part of the luggage was gone, Mrs. Duffy took hold of one end
of the trunk, and, telling Annie to lift the other,
both carried it into a long, wide, dreary-looking
structure not unlike the arch of a wooden bridge.
They then joined the stream, filing into another
part of the building, on through a number of narrow
doors, at one of which they were obliged to give
their names, then into a large open space, like an
old-country market-house, filled with emigrants,
some walking dreamily to and fro, and others
lying on the cold flags to rest their weary
limbs.   A number of licensed boarding-house

keepers, or "sharks," as they are called in New York, were going amongst them, seeking to entice as many as they could to their establishments for the night.

Now, we think it is very right and proper to allow the keepers of respectable lodging-houses to enter Castle Garden ; for many poor emigrants, who are weary and anxious to find a bed to rest on, know not where to look for it. But to permit such unscrupulous, heartless villains as are usually found there to lead away innocent, unsuspecting people to their dens is a standing shame to the city. But we are greatly afraid that the first-mentioned class have a slender chance of that privilege till some change amongst the officials takes place.

At length, when the poor creatures were worn out with watching to be let out in the open air, a flashily dressed official mounted a platform, and began to call out the names of such as had letters awaiting them. The number of letters was not many, but the time he occupied in read-ing the addresses was intolerable. Not that he was by any means a slow reader ; for he mentioned a name so quickly, driving Christian and surname into one, that few of his listeners could make out what he said. The attention he bestowed on his dress, adjusting his collar smoothing down his bosom, and brushing up his hair after every name seemed to be the very object for which he was there. Many of the letters were thrown aside, no one claiming them, while the very persons for whom they were intended were in a fever of expectation on the floor.

This task over, such of the emigrants as chose were permitted to depart. Many availed themselves of this opportunity; but a few lonely, dejected creatures remained behind, hoping to find employment through the Free Labor Bureau. Annie, accompanied by Mrs. Duffy and her little boy, went in search of the nearest way to the part of the city where Kitty Brady lived, which, after many enquiries and long travelling, they found. It was a long way up the city; and, after an affectionate parting, and each promising to write to the other, Annie went aboard a street-car, and was driven off. Mrs. Duffy stood looking after her till the car was out of sight; then began making her own enquiries, and. being successful in these too, started for the Chambers Street ferry.

CHAPTER XV.

MEETING OLD FRIENDS, AGREEABLE AND OTHERWISE.

THE street-car jingled along merrily, first down a narrow, crowded street, filled with shops, outside and inside of which hung more ready-made clothing than Annie thought would supply half the world, then into a long, wide thoroughfare of much better appearance. Up this street, past more clothing-houses, with figures of men and women clad in the height of fashion dangling from the awnings; and underneath, on the sidewalk, Jews and Jewesses, old and young, some gesticulating frantically at the passers-by to "walk in" and purchase; others, pale and worn out from incessant talking, leaned against the windows, looking no more like life than the figures above their heads. Past oyster and beer saloons, with fat, lazy Dutchmen resting on the counters or sitting by the doors, while a few sat around a table drawn near the entrance, drinking, smoking, and playing cards. Past liquor-stores, looking very shabby and unwashed, with numbers of red-faced,

bloated, stupid-looking, ill-clad men dozing on barrels outside, and a few dandily-dressed fellows smoking cigars or chewing tobacco inside the. doors. Occasionally a youth or two, evidently taking the dry-rot, roused up one of the sleepers, and engaged him in conversation. Past peanut-stands, with Chinamen or Japanese sitting on the flags behind them. Up, up, on, on, till Annie thought she would never reach the end of the street. At length the car-conductor beckoned to her, and told her she was to get off at the next corner. He told her very kindly the way to take from there, and to watch the numbers on the doors. She thanked him, and, the car being stopped, got off, and after a short walk arrived at the house bearing the number she sought. She descended to the basement door, and rang the bell. A very cleanly-looking girl opened it, and asked politely whom she wanted to see.

" Please tell me is this where Kitty Brady lives ?" asked Annie.

" Yes," replied the other, " but she is out to market. Please step inside ; she'll be in directly."

Annie thanked her, and walked into the hall.

" Come on this way," said the other, going before, " and take a seat ; you look tired."

Annie followed her into the apartment, and being handed a chair, sat some time in silence :

for the girl seemed to be busy. At length the
door-bell jingled loudly.

"Here she is now," said the other; and, going
to the door, returned with a neatly-dressed, bright-
eyed, intelligent-looking girl, who looked so totally unlike the Kitty Brady she remembered
that she could not believe it was the same, till
the other girl said:

"Kitty, this young lady has been waiting to
see you."

Kitty, who had not the least idea of who Annie
might be, and was about to go up-stairs to her
duties, turned back, and, coming close to her,
looked into her face. Annie's eyes met hers,
and for a moment they looked into each other's
faces.

At length Annie burst into tears, and said sorrowfully: "You don't remember me, Kitty?"

This was the first time Annie had spoken. The
voice was enough—the same sweet voice Kitty
had heard a thousand times in her mother's
cabin.

"O little Annie, darling, dear! And can this
be you?" exclaimed Kitty, throwing her arms
around her neck.

They kissed each other again and again, and
wept till their faces were wet. Neither could
speak a word for some minutes. When Kitty sat

down by her new-found friend, and took her hand in hers, the other girl came and kissed her, too, and hoped they would always be good friends.

"I will not ask you anything further about home," said Kitty, when she had wept bitterly over the misfortune that had befallen Farrell Reilly's family, "till we go to my aunt's. I'll get leave to go with you for this evening."

Kitty dried her eyes as well as she could, and ran up-stairs, taking with her the parcel her mother had sent her, and soon returned with word she could spend the evening with her. Both girls started out, Annie feeling much happier than she thought she could in many a day.

After a pretty long walk, they reached the house. It was a neat, two-story frame building, with very white walls and very green Venetian blinds, and had a trim little garden in front. On the door was a highly polished brass plate bearing the name, Patrick Sweeny. Patrick Sweeny was the husband of Kitty's aunt, and, being a very sober, industrious mechanic, had by this time accumulated money enough to purchase the cottage and live comfortably. Kitty rang the bell, and the door was opened by a plainly-dressed, good-natured-looking, middle-aged woman, who kissed her niece affectionately, and then began chiding her for staying away so long. Kitty made the best excuse she could, and, turning to Annie, said:

"Aunt, if you were to think for the length of a day, I don't believe you would find out who this is."

"I am sure of that, child," said Mrs. Sweeny. "I have never, I think, seen the young lady before." And she looked kindly at Annie.

"Well, I'll not keep you waiting, aunt. She is Farrell Reilly's daughter Annie, just landed to-day."

"Farrell Reilly's daughter!" exclaimed Mrs. Sweeny, taking her by the hand, and kissing her fondly. "You are a thousand welcomes to my house. I am delighted to see one of your family under my roof." And she pushed the parlor door open, and led the girls inside, hastily removed Annie's hat and shawl, and sat down by her on the sofa. "And how is your father and mother, my child? 'Tis very strange, but I was dreaming of the old country last night; such a queer, mixed-up dream it was. Ryan, or John the Pig, as we used to call him, was in it, and Father Fitzpatrick, and your mother, and a strange young lady, whom I think must be you."

"'Twas, indeed, a very strange dream, aunt,' said Kitty. "Ryan is the cause of Annie being in New York to-day."

Mrs Sweeny raised her hands in alarm, and said :

" Tell me, Annie, did you leave your father and mother well ?"

" As well as could be expected, after what had happened to them," said Annie, her tears beginning to fall afresh.

Mrs. Sweeny was truly grieved when she heard the poor girl's story.

" Poor Farrell Reilly !" she said, putting her handkerchief to her eyes, " that was such a good friend to us all. How heart-sorry I am for his trouble ! I never dream of that scoundrel Ryan," she went on, " but something is sure to follow— either some trouble to ourselves, or I'll hear bad news. You may not have heard it, child, but he was the cause of our downfall in the old country. But now, when I look back, I think it may all have been for the best ; and you, too, child," drying Annie's tears, " will, I trust in God, live to say the same ; so we'll fret no more, and be as merry as we can."

" That's just the way to be, aunt," said Kitty.

" I couldn't help crying, either, when I heard it ; so we'll talk about something else."

By-and-by Mrs. Sweeny's daughter, a tall, handsome girl of about sixteen, came in, and all four spent a pleasant evening till it was time for Kitty

to leave. Annie and Miss Sweeny accompanied
her the greater part of the way, and, after receiving her word that she would call the following
day, turned back. They had not proceeded far,
when Miss Sweeny, happening to look across the
street, saw the figure of a man, buttoned up in a
long, close-fitting, white duster, with his back towards them, leaning against a lamp-post. He
was such a long figure, and such an awkward one,
that she could not help pointing him out to
Annie, and both smiled. As they approached,
however, Annie's smile quickly faded ; for on the
head of the figure she recognized the old glazed,
chipped cap of the Scotchman. Not wishing to
betray her feelings to her companion, and thinking after all it might not be he, she merely
moved a little closer to the other, and walked
on. Try as she might, she could not help cast-
ing a look in the direction of the lamp-post when
they came opposite to it, and there, sure enough
stood the graceful Scotchman, with his dull eyes
fixed on her as they used to be on board the
ship. He moved as if to come towards them, and
Annie, her heart throbbing violently, caught her
friend by the arm, and begged her to hurry on.

" Why, what's the cause of this, Miss Reilly ?"
asked the other, with a surprised look. " What
has happened to alarm you ?"

Annie cast a furtive glance at the Scotchman, who began walking along the opposite side, and said:

"Please don't ask me now. I'll tell you when we reach the house. Please hurry on."

Both girls began to walk quickly; but, when they quickened their pace, the man on the other side of the street did the same, jolting along, swaying from side to side, like an ill-built load of hay. Annie, thoroughly frightened, glanced at him occasionally, and at last begged Miss Sweeny to run. The latter, at length comprehending the cause of Annie's fright, broke into a laugh, and said:

"Now, Miss Reilly, you must not be so easily alarmed as that, or you cannot well live in New York. You will see more frights than him before a week."

At this moment, their annoyer hastened into the street, and, hurrying across, met them on a corner, despite all their efforts to get past before him.

"Ah! noo, lassie, you're nae kind to run away from an auld acquaintance," said he, planting himself before Annie. "I hae lang been watchin to see ye."

"I don't want to see you," said Annie, her terror giving her courage. "How dare you annoy me this way! Let me pass now, or I'll call the police."

" Nae, nae, noo," said he coaxingly ; "ye wad nae do that."

"I shall, I shall. Miss Sweeny, I beg of you call a policeman," said Annie.

That young lady had her face partly turned away, looking in the direction of a number of mechanics who were leaving a building on the opposite corner. She seemed not to hear Annie's entreaty, and still watched the men coming into the street, and scattering in every direction. At length a tall, straight, smart-looking young man came out, putting on his coat as he did so. Miss Sweeny quickly beckoned him, and in a second he was beside them.

" Here is a ruffian annoying this young lady," said Miss Sweeny, pointing to the Scotchman. " He has stopped her on the sidewalk."

The young man cast a scornful look on him, and, drawing his open hand, slapped him two or three times on each jaw ; and, when he turned to run, which was as quickly as he possibly could, gave him such a kick that for the first few yards he never made such speed in his life. Now, whether it were that the blows blinded his eyes, or that his feet were so very clumsy that they could not be trusted in a long race, we don't pre-

sume to know ; but, after running a little distance.
he stumbled and fell in a heap on a pile of dirt
which the sweepers had just gathered up.   A
policeman, happening to see the crowd of boys gath
ering around him, hurried up, and, in spite of all
his entreaties and declarations, hauled him off to
the station-house for a drunken man.   The policeman was not much to blame ; for he certainly
looked as if he had rolled the streets for a mile.

All this happened in such rapid succession that
Annie and her friend were bewildered.   The
young man accompanied them part of the way
towards the house, and, when he turned away,
Miss Sweeny told Annie he was Kitty's lover.

Mr. Sweeny was within, anxiously awaiting
their return ; for, after all he had heard his wife
say of Annie's family, he longed to see her.   He
was a low-sized, fat, good-humored-looking man,
with a merry twinkle in his eye, and just as fond
of fun as any Irishman in New York.   He told
so many amusing stories, and laughed so much
during the evening, that Annie thought that he
must be the happiest man in the world.   And he
was happy.   Strictly temperate from the day he
came to New York, he spent none of his money
in the grog-shop ; never came home cross, peev-
ish, or full of bad whisky, but always light-
hearted, even after the hardest day's toil, to join

his wife in their evening prayers; never lounged around dirty and slovenly on Sunday morning, but could be seen early in his seat at church. Through his industry and good habits, he was now independent.

Annie spent a very pleasant evening, went to rest on a comfortable bed, and slept soundly till the bright rays of the sun, shining through the blinds, told her the morning was far advanced.

CHAPTER XVI.

JAMES O'ROURKE'S EXPERIENCES IN A NEW YORK MENAGERIE.

AMES O'ROURKE continued to work along shore for several months, saving up all the money he could, and sending it to his father. He had written to Annie the day after his arrival, but, receiving word from Francis that she had gone to New York, tried by every possible means to learn her whereabouts in the city. He went to Castle Garden, hoping to receive some information in that very correct establishment; but no such name had been entered on the books about the time he mentioned. This he gleaned from a clerk after a day's delay—the very clerk to whom Annie had given her name. He even advertised in some of the daily papers, but without effect. When his hard day's work would be over, he went around to the houses of such as he had learned were from that part of Ireland, and requested them to make every enquiry; but months went by, and he heard nothing of Annie. The

only conclusion he could arrive at was that she had gone on to some distant city.

This bitter disappointment weighed heavily on his mind. If she were in Ireland, where he might hear from her now and then, he would not have felt so heart-broken; but to know she had been and probably was in New York, that perhaps he saw the ship that carried her over coming into the harbor, and that every effort of his to see her or hear of her proved in vain, was painfully distressing.

Meanwhile, the class of people amongst whom he was thrown were not calculated much to improve his spirits. We do not mean by this his fellow-laborers, who were for the most part honest, hard-working men like Terence McManus. The latter had told James, when he first went to work, that he could board with him if he chose; but O'Rourke knowing, from the limited accommodation he possessed, that this offer was prompted only by goodness of heart, sought out another boarding-place—an act which he very soon after regretted.

This establishment stood in one of the side streets, directly over a beer-saloon. It consisted of three floors, divided into five or six rooms each, and served no fewer than fifty boarders. That these rooms were of small compass need

not be told. Those which looked out on the
street or into the yard in the rear were the lar-
gest, and contained two and three beds each. The
middle bedrooms were of such small dimensions,
and the doors leading into them were so narrow, that the beds they contained must have
been built there. These were sometimes called
the dark bedrooms—a most appropriate name ;
for, except the door is open or broken down, as
sometimes happens, not a ray of light can enter
them. We defy any man, even the most unim-
aginative, to sleep there one night without thinking of dungeons, skeletons, and ghosts.

All the floors were bare but clean, except
where covered with tobacco-juice or the ashes of
pipes. The beds—well, one of them would not
be the most soothing place in the world for an ill-
tempered man with the toothache. The straw
or hay, or whatever it might be, had an obstinate
habit of getting into hard, round lumps, which,
if you tried to smooth down in one spot, instantly
burst up in another. The first night a person
sleeps on one of those beds he is sure to start up
with the impression that some one is beating him
about the ribs ; and, to complete the comfort of
the thing, the pillows are hard enough for the
head and neck of any patriarch.

The kitchen was on the lowest floor in the rear,

and so hot and fierce did it look from the front room that the most stout-hearted boarder never ventured to enter it during the warm weather.

The first evening James came to the establishment, the boarders were assembled at supper, and the lamp on the table burned very dimly. A first glance along the row of faces, and his heart sank as he thought of Liverpool; but when he was seated, and surveyed them more closely, he saw that every man had his hands and face washed. This must have taken considerable time; for James saw but one wash-stand in the hall, and one towel sewed together at the ends, which turned on a round piece of wood like a weaver's reeling-stick.

The boarding-mistress, Mrs. Grady, stood at a small, narrow table by the window, on which were placed two such large dishes of corned beef and soup that James wondered how they maintained their balance, busily engaged serving out their contents. On the table were pickles, radishes, tomatoes, onions, cheese, butter, and baker's bread in every variety of shape, but all in very small quantities, and so close together in the centre of the table that it must have required extraordinary exertions on the part of those at the ends to reach them at all.

Mrs Grady's object in thus placing them may

probably have been a very laudable one. Her husband, a small, weazen, crabbed-looking fellow, who was what is commonly called a " curbstone broker," or vagabond real-estate agent, always sat at the middle of the table, and she may have been determined to give him sufficient, no matter who wanted.

The swarm of flies on and around the table was something awful. Bread, butter, boarders' hands and arms, meat, soup, eyes, noses, and sometimes mouths were infested with them; and the increased hum they kept up seemed to prevent Mrs. Grady hearing any boarder who happened to want his plate replenished.

James felt nearly as much disgusted as he had been in Liverpool, and ate very little supper, hurried outside, and went down to the docks to catch a little fresh air from the river.

When he returned, the boarders were about to go to bed, and Mrs. Grady pointed out to James his bedfellow while he remained in the house : " A very nice, clean man," she explained. O'Rourke looked at his hollow, drunken eyes and old, torn red shirt, and gravely doubted the good lady's recommendation.

James sat for some time at the window, looking at a wrangling crowd of Dutchmen outside the saloon, one of whom kept continually shout-

ing, "Vat for you do mit das, ha? Vat for you
do, ha? Vat for you, oder any man, in the city of
Ni Yorik, dare exult me oder mine olt voomans?"

When he had roared himself hoarse, and no
one appeared to show cause why himself or his
wife should be insulted, he muttered a few
drunken curses at a crowd of boys who had
gathered around himself and his comrades, and
staggered into the saloon again.

James left the window and went up-stairs to
his room, which, by the way, was one of the dark
bedrooms. As he approached the door, a faint
light, dimly visible through the keyhole, attracted
his attention. He pushed open the door, and
there, lying on his back in the middle of the bed,
with all his clothing, shoes included, on, was his
new comrade, quietly smoking a long white pipe.
James thought this a novel place to smoke in,
but he merely threw the door open; for, from
the close heat of the room and the fumes of the
tobacco, the apartment was well-nigh suffocating.

He sat down on his trunk—the only seat, except the bed, in the room—and began taking off
his shoes, hoping the smoker would leave the
bed, that he might lie down. But, no; he lay
there, lamenting the high price of liquor, and
predicting the consequent ruin of the country,
till his pipe was smoked down, when he turned

over on his side, and, pulling a paper of tobacco from underneath the bolster, began to refill it, which having done, he dived after a match in his old, torn vest, lighted it on his thigh, and went on smoking as before.

James's patience was exhausted, and he said : " Do you intend smoking all night ? If you do, you had better sit outside here, and let me lie down."

" Augh ! the divil a bit hurry I am in to go to bed," said he. " Me and a couple more got a little bit tight around noon-time, and the boss sacked every man of us; so I am not goin' to work in the mornin'."

"Well, I am not so," said James. " I want to go to bed. It wasn't on your account I spoke. I assure you."

The other kept silent, and smoked away.

"Stand up and leave that pipe away ! I wonder how you can tolerate the smell of it yourself; I am sick half an hour ago."

" Arrah ! take it aisy, can't ye ?" said he. " I'll be through now in twinty minutes."

" Up with you to your feet !" exclaimed O'Rourke, losing all patience ; and, catching him by the shoulder, he lifted him to his feet, and left him standing on the floor. "If I have the misfortune to be in the same room with you any

more, I'd recommend you to quit smoking in
bed."

"All right, I'll get square one of these days,
me lad. I'm the ouldest boorther in this house,
and ought to have the same privilege as any
other man; but I'll get *square*." And he sat
down so heavily on the other's trunk as almost
to crack the lid.

"If you break my trunk, I'll *flatten* you," said
James, as he searched for a peg to hang his
clothes on.

"I want me rights," said the other, with a
drunken leer, and raising his left shoulder to his
ear.

"What rights?" asked James.

"The same as other men," he shouted, waving
nis hand toward the other rooms.

James looked out and saw at least a dozen
boarders, some outside, some inside the bed-
clothes, while the smoke from their pipes was
struggling desperately to escape through a broken
pane.

He threw himself on the bed, and, having
worked very hard that day, was soon asleep.
Happening to wake up during the night, the
first object that met his eyes was the red glare
of his companion's pipe close by his face.

The next day he made enquiries after a new

boarding-house; but, being told by his fellow-laborers that they were all alike, he made up his mind, in case every effort to find Annie failed, to leave New York.

Every effort in that direction did fail, as our readers know. So when the demand for work-men at the oil-fields in Pennsylvania came, James and a few others set out there.

CHAPTER XVII.

ANNIE FALLS IN WITH A MOTHER-IN-LAW AND A TARTAR.—BOTH TRY TO CONVERT HER.

OTWITHSTANDING that Mr. and Mrs. Sweeny and Kitty Brady did all in their power to persuade Annie to take a few weeks' rest, she advertised for a situation in one of the morning papers the second day after her arrival in New York. Why she insisted on putting her name to the advertisement none of her friends could make out; but Annie had been thinking very much of James O'Rourke, and praying that she might see him, and that may have accounted for it.

In reply to the advertisement, a tall, thin-jawed, oldish-looking woman, with a net shawl drawn tightly around her shoulders, called about noon. Mrs. Sweeny happened to be out at the time, otherwise she would not have let Annie engage with her. But the latter was anxious to fulfil the promise she had made to Francis. This was the first answer to her advertisement she had received, so she answered the numerous questions put to her as well as she could, and was not a little delighted when the lady told her to come in the morning.

She left a name and address on a card, which she explained were not her own, but that of her married daughter, for whose service she had engaged Annie. The latter looked at the name—Mrs. Derby Granville Phillips—and thought to herself it was a pretty high-sounding name, but not such a strange one after all.

The address was Brooklyn, and this confused her a little at first, knowing it was so far from her friends in New York ; but that was not to be considered.

Accordingly, at the appointed hour in the morning, Annie appeared at the door of Mrs. D. G. Phillips, looking very pretty and cheerful at the prospect of soon being able to help her father and mother. The door was opened by the old lady who had hired her in New York, who, in return to Annie's nod of recognition, merely held up her hands very high, and said, as she pulled out a large watch with a very heavy chain, which Annie thought looked remarkably like brass :

"I like punctuality. You are just three minutes too soon ; but we'll overlook that for this time. Hurry down to your business."

Annie, not a little surprised at this odd reception, went down-stairs to the kitchen, and, seeing no

one there, stood for a moment, not rightly knowing what to do next. Soon she heard the tread
of feet coming down the stairs, and, looking along
the hall, saw a young lady, who in thirty years
hence would pass very easily for the old one,
coming towards her with a little white lap-dog
resting on one arm, and a very flashy novel in the
hand of the other. She put down the animal as
she entered the kitchen, and began talking to it
and fondling it, calling it the most endearing
names, and bending down occasionally to kiss it
and hug it to her breast.

She did not look towards Annie, or seem to
know she was present, till she had tired herself
caressing the dog, when she turned round suddenly, and said, with her mother's lofty scorn :

" You're the new servant, eh?"

" Yes, madam," replied Annie, her voice quivering.

" A nice servant you are!" said the other, holding an eye-glass, which only dimmed her sight, to
her eye, and, with her mouth drawn very tight.
looking at the poor girl. " Why don't you go up-
stairs and change your dress, 'm?"

" Please, madam," said Annie, " the other lady,
your mother I think—"

" Go on, go on ; don't stand to talk to *me* about
what you think. I am mistress here," said she

lifting the dog again. " Change your clothes, and look like work, quick."

" Where shall I change my clothes, please, madam ?" asked Annie.

" Well, well, my dear," was the reply. " Where is she to change her clothes? Have you ever been in a first-class house before ?" But without giving Annie time to answer, she added, throwing back her head, and closing her eyes languidly, " Go up to the servant's room on the top floor."

Annie went up-stairs, and, as she passed the front door, she was almost tempted to run into the street and away.

The servant's room of the " mansion," as Mrs. Phillips loved to call it, was a very miserable apartment ; the walls and floor bare, and the ceiling hardly five feet in height.

In getting ready for her work, no girl could make greater haste than she did but, on descending to the kitchen again, she was met by the angry frown of the mother-in-law, who declared she really thought Annie was gone and in New York by this time.

The mansion employed but one girl, and as the last one had been gone three or four days, and neither the mother nor daughter offered her the least assistance, Annie spent a very laborious morning. There was no system in the " mansion," which made the work even harder. Mrs. Phillips would call her from the range to smooth a collar, and from that, before it was finished, to run up-stairs or out to the shop for something she needed " desperately," as she always added, to hurry Annie.

Being so very busy did not annoy her, but everything she did was found fault with, and when she expected a smile, received only a withering frown.

Poor little Annie, her heart was almost breaking; but she thought of the calm evening by the river's bank in far-off Ireland, when James said she was brave as a little lion, and she did not shed a tear now either.

During the afternoon, Mrs. Phillips's two little boys came in from school, and, seeing the new servant, were delighted at the opportunity it gave them to display their polite training.

" Halloo !" cried the eldest, a youth of about seven, with a yellowish, unwholesome-looking face, narrow forehead, and very flat nose—" hallo ! And when did you come ?" And he ran up to Annie, who was lifting a large vessel, filled with hot water, from the range, and deliberately walked across her toes.

" Beware, beware, Gussy, of the scalding water !" cried his grandmother, who happened to come in at the moment. "What a darn j lad you are!"

"None of your business," said the hopefu boy. "She is *our* servant, not yours."

"O Gussy!" said the old lady, who, by the way, was only tolerated in the house. "I mean the risk you have just run of getting the boiling water over you, that's all."

"Keep your talk to yourself," said the youngest youth. "Papa told you and mamma told you to interfere with us no more, or you might go some place else."

"Say, when did you come?" asked the eldest again, moving beside Annie.

She made no reply, but went on with her work.

"Oh! she's stuck up, she is," said the youngest, throwing a smoothing-iron into the water, causing it to splash up on the poor girl's face and arms.

Annie turned to the old lady, and said, while her lips quivered:

"Pray, madam, tell them to cease tormenting me this way."

"Ha! ha!" laughed both. "Her tell us to stop. She has no more right here than you have yourself," said the oldest.

"But come along, Roy; papa will murder us for keeping her idle."

And the two scampered up-stairs, and amused their mother, first by relating to her the tricks which "Gussie had played on the new girl," and again exciting her wrath by telling her that their grandmother had interfered with them.

At nightfall, Mr. D. G. Phillips came home. He was a small, thin, cross-grained man, with an immense black mustache and a bald head. Not a bald head of the ordinary kind, however, for we dare say the owner of the "mansion" would scorn that : but a crown dotted over with bare spots here and there, which, if put together, would leave a clear space extending probably to the backs of his ears.

Annie opened the door for him, and he shot inside with such force that she peeped through the glass to see if any person outside pitched him in. When she looked around, he had disappeared into the parlor, and she could hear the ring of Mrs. Phillips's voice as she rated him for not being home sooner. Annie hurried down to her duties, dreading lest she might hear a word not intended for her ears ; but as we are not so scrupulous, we will stop a moment and see the cause of the row.

"A pretty time of night for you to come landing home," said Mrs. Phillips, closing the novel she had been reading, as her husband put his head inside the parlor door.

"What are you talking about night for?" said the husband, throwing himself on the worn sofa. "Are you prepared for me this evening again?"

"Yes, sir; I am prepared for you," said Mrs Phillips, coming close, and looking down on him with a frown. "I want to know where you were till this time of night—night, I repeat. I know I can't believe a word you say, but I insist on some answer."

"Business in the office delayed me," said he, with an ominous look, at which Mrs. Phillips smiled scornfully. "And don't tell me I am a liar again. It ill becomes you to call any one a liar. Your mother, rot her, is the biggest."

"I'll not tolerate this, sir," exclaimed she, stamping her foot and interrupting him. "If anything is to be said to mother, I'll say it."

"But this is my house," said he modestly.

"Is it your house? Oh! to be sure it is. I am no better than a servant here," said she, with an hysterical laugh. "And of course you can come in or go out any hour of the night you like."

"Why not?" said he.

"Why not!" echoed she with a yell that brought the old lady up-stairs in a second. "Oh! what treatment for me to bear. He openly tells me, mother," continued she, in the same loud voice, "that he'll come home when he likes, and go out

at night when he likes." Here a flood of tears
choked her utterance.

"I'd put the seas between me and him," said
the mother-in-law, shaking her head furiously at
him.

"Merciful God, if I only could!" said the son-
in-law, in an undertone.

"Lettie, dear, I'll run for some cold water; I
think you're going to faint," said her mother.

"Oh! don't leave the room now, I beg of you,"
exclaimed the sobbing lady.

"Oh! dear, oh! dear. Bless my soul, he has a
very villanous look on him this evening," said the
old lady, turning back and looking at her son-in-
law, who certainly did not look very agreeable, with
his face, mustache, and forehead puckered up with
an expression of deep pain. "Oh! my soul and
body," continued the kind-hearted old lady, wringing her hands, "was it for this I raised and edu-
cated—ahem!—my daughter in the best style?"

She seemed to expect an answer to this important enquiry from some person hidden up in the
ceiling; for she walked the floor a dozen times,
her eyes turned upwards, repeating the same
question.

The expression on the husband's face grew
worse as he watched her, and his wife's tears fell
very plentifully and comfortably, as she sat on a

chair opposite her husband, with her head turned away from him. .

" If I were you, I'd put the ocean between us," said the old lady again, improving on her favorite expression. " Let us pack up now, my dear."

Mrs. Phillips dried her tears instantly, and, springing to her feet, ordered her mother to leave the room.

" What business have you in the parlor?" taking her by the shoulders. " Go down-stairs, and wait till you're sent for."

As the worthy daughter turned from the door after putting her mother outside, she thought, by the altered look of her husband, that he was pleased with what she had done. And as please him was the very last thing on earth she could think of, she burst into tears again, and called him a brute, a wretch with a heart like flint or steel, and numerous other choice names. Mr. Phillips bore all patiently till her voice grew hoarse, when she took the little dog in her arms, and went up-stairs.

At length Sunday morning came, and there was a great bustle of preparation in the " mansion." A celebrated divine of Brooklyn, Rev. Dr. Brassman, was to preach in the Academy of Music that Sabbath. He was the family pastor, and a great favorite with Mrs. Phillips.

Annie worked very hard during the morning, assisting them, and, when they were just ready to go out, the mother-in-law looked at her watch, and announced they were half an hour too early ; and as Mrs. Phillips detected a long delay in church, except her favorite preacher was there to entertain her, they sat down to wait till the proper time.

Now, the old lady was one of those very sensible people who try and make the very best use of every moment. The thought that now might be a favorable opportunity to convert Annie came into her head. She ventured to tell her son-in-law and daughter of it, and was greatly delighted, good soul, to find they did not snub her.

The three were seated in the parlor, with the two boys tumbling over each other on the floor beside them. Mrs. Phillips held the little white dog in her arms, and the old lady sat bolt upright, waving an immense black fan.

The bell rang, and Annie appeared, looking very pale and beautiful, having just dressed herself to go out to church.

" Ahem ! Come nearer us here," said the old lady, putting on her glasses. " We want to talk a little with you now that we have time."

Annie approached, wondering greatly what the cause of this solemn council could be.

"You're a Romanist, an't you?" began the old lady.

"I am a Roman Catholic, madam," said Annie, her face flushing.

"Ah! yes; the greater part of you Irish are," said the other. "But don't you know you are astray?"

"No, madam, I do not," said Annie. "The Catholic Church was established by our Lord himself."

"Nonsense, nonsense," said the other, with a toss of her head and fan, "impossible—the Catholic Church founded by Christ! Have you ever read the Bible?"

"Certainly, madam," replied Annie; "it was the first book I learned to read."

"Don't tell me that, girl," said the old lady, looking round on the others. "Your priests forbid you to read the Bible; I know it."

"With due respect for your knowledge, madam," said Annie politely, "our priests do no such thing! They earnestly recommend every Catholic to read the Bible, but it must be the Bible complete and unadulterated."

"This is something new for us," said the mother-in-law.

"It is by no means new, madam," replied Annie, "but it is something very new and strange

to me to hear any one assert that priests forbid
the use of the Bible. Our parish priest in Ireland, so anxious was he every family should have
a Bible, that he supplied those himself who were
unable to purchase one."

"I should think that a very dangerous game for
himself," said Mrs. Phillips, patting the dog's head.

"How, madam, may I ask?" said the girl.

"Why, then you would all see the folly of his
pretensions," was the reply. "The Bible doesn't
tell you he can forgive your sins?"

"Certainly not," said Annie, "by any power
of his own."

"And by whose power, then?" put in Phillips,
who thought he had been long enough silent.

"By the power of God, who has given them
that authority," said Annie.

"Oh! they all say that," said the mother-in-
law with a sneer. "Listen to *me*, young woman,"
she added earnestly. "Do you think, because our
Lord promised that power to his apostles, whom
he saw and conversed with every day, that your
priests now, after the lapse of eighteen hundred
years, possess the same power?"

"I believe," said Annie, with something of a
smile on her face, "that our Lord can do now
what he did eighteen hundred years ago. Time
has not diminished his power."

" I—I know that," said the old lady, fidgeting uneasily in her chair; "but what I mean to say is, he gave that authority to his disciples only."

" There is no reason for saying or thinking so," said Annie. " Those who lived at that time were not a privileged people, more than that they happened to be on earth at the same time as our Saviour. He came to save all—not one generation—and to grant all salvation through the same means."

The mother-in-law was biting her lip and twisting her fingers, thinking of what she would say next, when Mrs. Phillips joined in with:

" Then that is a very easy way to reach heaven —act as you like, and then go to your priest and get forgiveness."

" Oh! no," said Annie; " there are conditions necessary for a good confession."

" What are they?" asked the mother-in-law.

" The most important are," said the girl, "a sincere sorrow for the faults committed, and a strong resolution to sin no more."

" Ah!" said the old lady, pitching her head forward, " I have you now. You say our Lord came to save all, and yet you believe all except Catholics will be lost."

" What I said was," replied Annie, " that our Lord came to redeem all through the same means.

He did not adopt two methods; and I say now that the Catholic Church only preserves the Scriptures unchanged."

"Oh! yes, indeed," said Mrs. Phillips spitefully, "that's more of your priests' slander. I don't believe they do a thing else in their chapels on Sunday but abuse other people."

"You do our clergy a great injustice, madam," said the girl warmly, "when you say so. They preach the Gospel to their hearers, pointing out to them the evils they are to avoid and the virtues they should practise. Now, slander is a very great vice, and none is more severely condemned by our priests."

"Ha! but they tell you all Protestants will go to hell, don't they?" asked the old lady, taking up the thread of the argument.

"If you were to go to any of our churches on Sunday," said Annie, "you would think there was but one religion in the world; because our priests instruct their people in the doctrines of their own, and never mention the name of Protestant or any others who differ from us."

The mother-in-law drew out her broad-faced watch, and, to her great relief, saw it was time to go and hear the Rev. Dr. Brassman; so she told Annie that at some future period she would convince her of her error.

CHAPTER XVIII.

A MODERN CLERGYMAN.—REV. DR. BRASSMAN'S GREAT ENTERPRISE.

HE Rev. Dr. Brassman was a very indefatigable man, not alone in the service of God, but in his efforts to make a name here on earth. The Rev. Dr. knew as well as, perhaps, any minister that the apostles were poor and lowly men who cared not for this world's fame; but thinking that, as the world grows older, men grow wiser, the same poverty and humility were not expected from him. That the apostles preached to large multitudes he had no doubt, but saw that the language which gathered large crowds in those days would leave him an empty church now.

Of this he was more fully convinced by the example of a brother divine, who totally ignored Gospel preaching in his pulpit, and delighted his hearers with other and more entertaining information. In this he was very successful, as the number and respectability of his congregation went to show. At this, Dr. Brassman, as became a pious and charitable minister, grew very envious, and resolved, at all hazards, not to be kept in the background.

Dr. Brassman was a very eloquent gentleman, and had a powerful voice. Even in his calmest days, before the desire to become notorious laid hold of him, no nervous man or woman who happened to know his church would venture past while he was in the pulpit.

The dogs in that neighborhood had acquired such a habit of barking incessantly on Sunday evenings that every sensible citizen kept his canine muzzled on that day.

But when the desire to outvie his celebrated brother took possession of his head and lungs, the streets in his vicinity began to depopulate, and what people had nerve enough to remain put their dogs into the cellar before the terrible roar broke upon the air.

Now, it may seem strange how any one, except they were born deaf as a stone, could stand their ground inside the church, while the noise affected men and animals outside so much. Well, to any man or woman who may be disposed to doubt these truthful lines, we say—and he may go and try it, if he chooses—that it is much easier to withstand the yells of a roaring minister inside his temple than without.

When Mr. Phillips and his wife and mother-in-

law reached the Academy, they found the worthy
minister already in the pulpit. This was a great
relief to the old lady; for, after the indifferent suc-
cess she had achieved in the controversy with
Annie, she wanted something to distract her
thoughts. The doctor had not commenced speaking yet, and sat on a low seat within the pulpit,
his chin resting on its edge, looking placidly on
the thickening crowd. His head, which was all
of him that could be seen, was a very peculiar
one indeed—very short and small behind, bulged
out alarmingly over each ear, and very narrow on
the crown. His face was very long and straight,
eyes large and watery, nose short and turned
down, and forehead surprisingly high and narrow. When he saw every seat filled, he rose
slowly and with dignity, pushed his hair up in
front till it stood on ends, looked wildly around,
and, striking the side of the pulpit heavily with
his open hand till the building echoed again, said,
in a heavy undertone:

"Brothers, we *air* here *toe*-day"—puckers up
his mouth, throws back his chest, and shakes his
head—"saints and sinners. The little bird that
tunes its lay toe heaven speaks *a* lesson of wisdom toe us all toe-day." A little higher: "Why
does that little bird sing? Because"—louder—
"it is free; free, my brethren, toe hop from branch

to branch "—sorrowfully—" and gather up for its young the tiny little worm. Again "—his very loudest—" I ask, Why does that little bird sing? Becau—au—au—ause it has a free conscience," smiting the pulpit again. " Becau—au—au—ause it is no thief who steals. Becau—au—au—ause it is no liar who breeds discord. Becau—au—au—ause it is no drunkard who comes home late at night." (Mrs. Phillips nudged her husband) " Becau—au—au—ause that little bird is no murderer who shoots, or stabs, or beats out the brains of its fellow-man." (He stops and drinks; the mother-in-law is greatly affected.) " The beautiful parable—ahem! I made it myself—which I have told you about the little bird reminds me that in the city of New York, that hot-bed of sin, and crime, and *etarnal* drunkenness, *a* man lies condemned toe die. Great efforts, we hear, are being made by that man's friends toe save him; but "—a perfect scream—" what did the old law say?" stamping his foot, and swinging his arms wildly round: " *An* eye for *an* eye, *a* tooth for *a* tooth. My friends, it makes my heart sad when I see hardened sinners *going back* on the old law in this way. *Po-*litical *co-*ruption, my friends, is at the bottom of this and every other evil in the land. In the olden times, the pure old times, the people had no Bill Plunderfoots, no Dick

Bezzlers; and if they had, my brethren, what would they have done with them. Suppose, my brethren, when Moses, that man of God and of decided opinions, was leading the chosen people through the bushes, and he had discerned *a* Bill Plunderfoot in the camp, what would that upright, uncompromising man," clasping his hands and looking upwards, "have done? I'll tell you what Moses, who knocked the ungodly Egyptian on the head, would have done. He'd have smote," shaking his fist like another Moses, "Bill Plunderfoot down—down intoe perdition straight away. If any man says toe any of you, my brethren, that Moses wouldn't have *come* out as I say, tell that vile man he *lies*." Grows furious. "Tell that scurvy man he's in error; tell that man he's on the broad road that leads toe death; tell that blind man he's going toe hell himself."

The learned doctor continued in this very edifying strain, occasionally varying his subject, for at least two hours, when he stopped as suddenly as if he were deprived of the power of speech, sat down in the pulpit so quickly that one might think he had lost the power of his limbs, and drank three glasses of brown water in succession. This was a warning to his flock that he intended making some very important announcement, so

they retained their seats. He sat for a few minutes, his head thrown back, eyes and mouth
closed tightly, breathing heavily through his
nostrils.

" Something staggering must be coming,"
whispered the mother-in-law to her daughter.

At length he rose, straight and slowly, like
steam ascending from a bottle, and, when he had
gained his full height, advanced to the edge of
the pulpit, and said:

" Brethren, speaking toe you of the old law in
the commencement of my sermon reminds me
now that we should practise *a* few of the ceremo-
nies of the times gone by. That fell destroyer
and mad, fierce, unrelenting fiend fire—fire, my
friends " (an old, unmarried lady near the pulpit
tries to faint, but fails, and three little girls scream)
—-" fire, my brethren, has destroyed our taber-
nacle wherein we used to all mingle our sweet
voices in salutation and praise. The old spot was
dear toe us all, and we long toe cover it with a
sacred roof again. You have all subscribed gen-
erously towards that object, but as yet we have
far from enough toe complete the task.

" Let us again turn our thoughts toe the little bird, toe all feathered creation, my brethren.
They build their nests now as they did *a* thousand
years ago, choose their mates as they did *a*

thousand years ago, and wear the same plumage now as they did *a* thousand years ago. Now, my friends, let us draw *a* moral from the feathered inhabitants of the aerial skies—*a* moral, my friends that will draw us some funds. From this congregation, brethren, I will select the most beautiful lady" (the old maid who had tried to faint now tried to smile) " and the handsomest young gentleman, and on to-morrow evening marry them in the good old costume of the seventeenth century, in the presence of as many as choose toe pay one dollar each admission."

" Hear! hear! Bravo! Bully for you! Hurrah," shouted the men, while the ladies waved their fans and handkerchiefs.

" I wish toe add," said the preacher, smiling, " that the marriage will not be binding except both are satisfied."

The old maid, who had risen to her feet in the excitement, threw herself back in her seat with a deep sigh, and the Rev. Dr. Brassman retired from the pulpit.

CHAPTER XIX.

JAMES O'ROURKE AT THE OIL-FIELDS.—A SKETCH OF HIS COMPANIONS.

HE Pennsylvania oil-fields were only a short time in operation when James O'Rourke and those who accompanied him arrived there. A number of rude huts, of rough, unplaned timber, were in course of construction for the accommodation of laborers, and one or two had just been completed. They were not built with much view to comfort, and were but poorly adapted to keep out the cold and storms of winter, which had already set in; but the air was pure, and this, after his experience in a city boarding-house, made James overlook every other disadvantage.

The men employed in the fields were from every part of America and Europe, and were for the most part a very reckless set of fellows, who cared for nothing but drinking, carousing, and fighting. But James kept apart from them as much as possible, taking no part in their conversation during the day, and in the evenings sitting alone by himself, thinking of home.

A source of great trouble to him was, he could hear of no chapel in that part of the country. He made repeated enquiries among the laborers, but none of them knew anything of such a place, or cared, to use the words of one," if there wasn't a chapel on the face of the earth."

The man who made this remark was a young Irishman only a few years from the old land. He had heard old vagabonds talk in this way, and thought it very manly to imitate them.

"You don't care if there wasn't a chapel in the world?" repeated James, with a look in which were blended scorn and pity.

" No ; why the divil should I ?" replied Dooley —for such was his name—stuffing half a paper of tobacco into his mouth.

" You are a Catholic, are you not ?" asked James.

" Yis ; they used to call me that in Ireland ; but I'm nothin' at all now."

" And why have you seen fit to change so much here ?" asked the other.

" Religion, I see, is only a humbug. I had very little sinse in Ireland. Augh, Lord ! sure the people there know nothin' at all." And he pushed the old cap to the back of his head, and tried to look very knowing.

" Am I to believe you are in earnest in what

you say?" asked James, looking at him atten-
tively—"believe that you, a young man not long
from Ireland, have completely turned your back
on the teachings of the Holy Catholic Church?"

" In troth, and 'pon me sowl, ye may shwear it
that I mane every word I say. I seen the toime
I thought the ground 'id open and swallow me
up for even thinkin' the loikes; but I tell ye, a
man soon gets brave in America."

" Do you call it bravery," asked James, " to
dread to acknowledge your creed, the creed of
your forefathers, because those around you despise religion? Brave! Why, you are the meanest
of all cowards!"

" What do I care what me forefathers belaved,
or what me father or mother belaves either. I
must look out for meself now. Phat's any one in
the world to me but meself?"

" If a dog could speak," said James angrily,
" I dare say he would say the very same thing.
He cares for no one but himself." But checking
his passion, he went on: " Surely you don't think
you'll thrive any the better here by turning your
back on your religion?"

" Divil a much meself cares for money," was
the answer, " if I can get a bit to ate, and a
dhrink of whisky while I am in it; that's all I
care for."

"So you're a drunkard, too," said James, nod-ding his head sorrowfully.

"I can sthand more gin on a Saturday night than any other man in the diggins," was the an-swer. "When I began to dhrink first," he went on, with a laugh, "I thought I'd niver be able to keep up to the rest ov the boys; it used to give me a headache; and thin I'd be thinkin' of phat ould Father Philip used to say about drunkards long ago, and phat me father and mother id think if they only hard it; but I soon got over that; and so will you too, me boy, come all right in the ind, and be one of the best fellahs in the fields one ov these days." And he slapped the other on the shoulder.

"Sit down again, and listen to me for a mo-ment," said James.

"Come and have something to dhrink; me throat's dhry afther so much talk," said the other.

"You know very well," said James, turning away his head, "I am no drinker. Have patience for a little."

"All right, young fellah, but don't say any-thing to make me drier, or I can't sthand it."

James did not heed this remark, but went on:

"You are a young man yet, and have the world before you; and just ask yourself the question, Is now not the proper time for you to prepare for old age? In these fields, and in every other work in America where a number of men are employed, how many are able to work? By right, not one-half. It is pitiful to see so many old, weakly, worn-out creatures, as I may call them, struggling to do hard labor, with possibly not five years of existence before them ; not one bit better than old horses. And what makes it sadder still is that the greater part of them have themselves only to blame for their misery. When they were strong, when work was no burden to them, they took care neither of themselves nor of their earnings ; ruining their health with bad whisky, for which they squandered their money."

" Ah, phat's life to a man without he has some pleasure?" said the other, interrupting him. " And I don't see anything else there's so much pleasure in as a glass of whisky."

" Pleasure?" said James. " Why, you were listening to that old man, that works in the gang with me, talking last night, were you not?"

" Phat old man? Oh ! yes—ould Mickey that was saying he's twenty-five years in the country But he's a mane whinger, anyway."

" He spends all his money the same as you do, at any rate," said James ; " and his shirt is no better or cleaner than your own."

" Ay, but," said the other, in an injured way,
" he takes the whole good out ov the thing by
cryin' over it."

" He knows," said James, " that in a very short
time he'll not be able to clutch the spade, and
that there is nothing before him but die of want.
The man has become an habitual drunkard, and
now is powerless to save himself. To advise or
reason with any one reduced to his state is useless ; but we can learn a lesson from his folly.
Drink, he tells us, is no longer a pleasure to
him ; 'tis a hell from which he cannot escape. It
has lowered him from the rank of a human being,
and left him nothing better than an animal. The
only feeling in his heart is regret."

" The divil a bit of me is ivir sorry," said the
other, in a careless way. " Whin the money's
gone, I say, let it go."

" Why, he says he felt in like manner when he
took to drink," said O'Rourke ; " or, to use his
own words, ' Was as light-hearted without a penny
as when he'd have fifty dollars in his pocket.'
But the man was strong to earn more then ; he
could not look forward to the day when that
strength would fail him."

" Augh ! I say,' replied Dooley, with a twist
of his body, " whin a man isn't fit to work, it
makes little matther what comes of him. He is

afther havin' his day; I wouldn't mind how I spint the last few years of me days, if toimes were good up to that."

" I little thought, of all people in the world,' said James, " that an Irishman could be found to use such an expression—to show himself so utte, ly wanting in every honorable feeling. Picture to yourself what you would then be, and what you will be if you don't take heed—scorned and despised by every one, crawling around, a thing with life in it, no more; a burden to yourself and to the world."

" Oh! be me sowl, its preachin' a sarmon ye are; and, as I don't care for lecthers. I'll go and have me whisky."

James looked sorrowfully after him, as his manly but ragged figure disappeared into the door of the little rum-shop, and thought to himself what a woful blight to his countrymen in America love of such places proved.

In a few days after the foregoing conversation a native of Pennsylvania State came to work in the fields; and from him O'Rourke learned that a long way off, beyond the blue hills, a chapel could be found. The following Saturday night, when the laborers were enjoying themselves as usual, he set off in the direction indicated, his heart full of joy at the prospect of hearing Mass in the morning.

CHAPTER XX.

STRANGE OCCURRENCES IN THE "MANSION."--
HAPPY LIFE OF A MOTHER-IN-LAW.—ANNIE
RECEIVES A LETTER FROM HOME.

ANNIE lived at the "mansion" a little
over a month, bearing patiently with
every hardship and insult, but always
bravely and intelligently defending her
race and creed against the repeated attacks of the
mother-in-law and her daughter.

She had written to her father and mother the
evening before leaving Patrick Sweeny's, giving a
long account of her voyage, and telling them
what great friends she met with on her arrival
in New York. With what anxiety she waited for
an answer, giving the ship which carried her note,
and the one that bore the reply, the shortest possible time to cross the ocean. From the hour
she expected the letter, till three days later, when
Kitty Brady walked in with it, a cheerful smile on
her face, Annie was in the height of grief, imagining the most terrible things had caused the delay.

It happened, fortunately, she was alone, the old
and young lady having gone out for a walk.

Annie caught the letter from Kitty's hand, and, recognizing her brother's writing, kissed the address fervently. Her hands trembled, and, dreading she would tear the letter in opening it, requested the other to open and read it for her. Kitty stood over by the window, and, with Annie's head resting on her shoulder looking down at the words, read as follows:

"AUGUST 15, 186–.

"MY DEAR, DEAR SISTER:

"To-day, the Feast of the Assumption, we besought the Queen of heaven to watch over you in a far-off land. This blessed day our prayers were all for you, Annie, at home and before the altar. Since you left us, this is the first time mother has been to the chapel; but to-day I assisted her there, that she might kneel at the Virgin's feet for our darling Annie. Since her return, she has felt much better than at any time since we lost our home. Father goes to the chapel every evening now, to pray for you, Annie. We were greatly delighted to learn from your letter that you reached the end of your long journey safely, and that you met with such friends in New York. God's blessing on all who are kind to poor, little, lonely Annie! O Annie dear! I thought my heart would break this morning when the procession

moved down from the altar, and your gentle face
was not amongst the bright throng. Of all your
friends here, not one is more sincerely sorry after
you than Mr. Lacy. When I meet him, his eyes
fill up, and he passes by without saying a word ;
and yet often when father and I are absent, he
comes to see mother, and talks to her of you.
Between him and Nancy Brady, she is recovering
quickly from the blow our double misfortune has
been to her. Nancy was extremely delighted to
hear your praise of Kitty's goodness to you.
She has taken it into her head now that Kitty
must come home and see her.

"The day after you left us, Annie, I went to
the castle, and found employment, and we are now
living in one of the little cottages I mentioned to
you that night by the pond. Martha's manner
towards mother was never worse than the day
you went away ; so I determined we should live
in her house as short a time as possible. Father
is greatly changed. He is no longer lively, and
walks about with his head down, speaking to or
noticing nobody. He had a habit of going out
very early in the morning the first week or so
after your departure. What he could be doing
abroad at that hour surprised me. So I followed
him one morning to the top of the demense hill
which you know overlooks our old home, where

he sat down on a stone, and, turning his eyes in that direction, began to cry. I begged him to tell me what brought him there. He told me he found great consolation in coming there, for he could look down on the old cottage, and picture you to himself walking in the little garden or in the green fields around. And, O Annie! at that moment I could not say he was doing wrong. The old, old, once happy home was before my eyes. I saw you as you used to stand by the door looking out on the river. The path leading to its banks, along which you and I so often ran, looked so familiar and friendly to me that your figure stood in its every winding. Soon my own eyes filled, and I again begged father to come away, but in vain. He desired me to return to mother, but mention nothing of where I had left him.

" Now, Annie, from what I have told you, you must not think we are very miserable here. True, our sorrow that you are gone from us is very great indeed, but your letter helped to calm it very much, now that you have the danger of the ocean over you.

" Now, sister, about your sending us help from there, let me tell you, and believe me, Annie, I am able to earn sufficient to keep us comfortably till you have supplied yourself with everything you need. And, Annie, when with God's help I have managed to leave father and mother a little something, I will go to you, and both of us will, I trust, be able then to keep them comfortable. I know, dear Annie, it is quite useless to remind you of what you owe to God, but you will pardon a brother's anxiety. I have done now, Annie, and pray the choicest blessings of Heaven may fall upon you. Father and mother send their blessings to you, Annie.

"Your loving brother,
"FRANCIS REILLY."

During the reading of the letter, poor Annie's tears fell incessantly; and Kitty, too, was so much affected that she was compelled to stop a few times to clear her eyes.

"Now, Annie," said she, handing the letter to her, "is not that much better news than you expected?"

"Oh! but think of their unhappy state with all," said Annie through her tears. "My poor mother, I know, will break her heart to see Francis working for any one; and my poor father— think of him wandering away to the hill-top at break of day to look down on the old home! When he takes the loss of it so much to heart, I'll soon hear of his death."

"Why, no, Annie," said Kitty; "your mother has better sense than fret over such a thing as Francis earning a living at the castle for a time, when you tell her how well he can do here, and the short time 'twill be till he's here with you. You see, Annie, how your people will do at home in a great measure depends upon how you get along here. Now, what a happiness 'twill be to you to have your brother here with you! Just think of that, and make it an object to be gained. Think how happy 'twill make your father and mother to receive good, cheerful letters from you. And when you are well, let them know; never tell them you are fretting; and if you have one true friend in the world, mention it to them. I say this to you now, Annie, because I know you will not delay in writing again, and 'twill make you so happy yourself to think you are making your people happy."

"God bless you," said Annie, kissing her friend, "for that good advice. I will write as cheering a letter as I can. But, Kitty, what do you say to your mother being anxious to have you pay her a visit? Do you intend going?"

"I'll think over that," said the other; "'tis a long time till summer yet. This is the first time mother has mentioned the like since I came to America. You must have said something about me in your letter that made her take such a notion."

Annie smiled, and was about to make some reply, when a violent ringing of the door-bell, again and again repeated, alarmed them. She ran to the door, and, when she opened it, the mother-in-law, her head very erect, and a tear in each eye, glided into the hall. Annie drew back into the parlor door; for the look and manner of the old lady was very alarming. She looked wildly up the stairs, ran to the head of the basement ones, held her ear downwards in a listening attitude, ran back, glared at the girl, and asked, as she shook her head fiercely:

"Has my daughter returned yet?"

"She has not," said Annie, moving further into the room. "I hope nothing is wrong, madam?"

"Don't question me; I don't tolerate it from a servant," was the kind reply. And she went to the door, and tried to look out through the glass. Annie did not venture to speak again; and, when she saw the old lady peering into the street, ran down and joined Kitty.

"I think I had better leave you now, Annie," said that young lady. "Don't neglect coming over on Sunday evening, and Miss Sweeny and you and I will go to Vespers together."

" Oh ! pray don't leave me alone here yet,'' said Annie earnestly. "Something is the matter with the old lady. She has just come in, and looks terrible. I would die here if you left me alone.''

" I'll wait a little while, then," said Kitty, " but not long.''

Another jingling of the bell, followed by a sharp kick on the outside of the door; Annie sprang to open it, and in came Mrs. Phillips, her face flushed, her mouth set, and her eyes fiery.

" Where is that old—" But catching a glimpse of her mother in the parlor, she dashed in, and shouted hoarsely, " How dare you, how dare you, I repeat, come into my house when I have expressly forbidden you to do so?''

" I'll explain to you, Lettie, if you only have patience, that 'twas all a mistake," said the mother, trembling.

" No explanation will do," said the other, stamping furiously, and scratching at her face. " You have done the job, and there's no remedy but prevent you ever getting ' a show ' to do the like again. Oh !'' and she wrung her hands, and champed her teeth, " to tell Mrs. Howard Roy Plantagenet that I worked in a factory in England !''

" Ah ! let me say one word, Lettie, just one,"

and the mother threw up her hands to keep her infuriated daughter back, " and then you'll see that wasn't what I said at all. You're the cause of all the shame yourself, to strike me with your parasol before so many ladies."

" You would, if you dare, you old disgrace, like to throw all the blame on me; but I am determined to get rid of you now." And—shall we record it?—catching her by the shoulder, " Here, now, leave my ' mansion ' this moment, and go into the streets, where you ought to be. The idea of me thinking to be as good as Mrs. Howard Roy Plantagenet or any other lady in the city, and keeping the like of you to tell my history to them!"

" I beg of you, my child, do not cast me out in my old days," pleaded the mother, turning her eyes, with a strange white look, on her daughter. " I don't deserve it of you."

"Oh! no," said the other, grinning into her face, " I suppose if *anybody* was here you'd tell them how you struggled in poverty and hunger to raise me, wouldn't you? Come on, now."

" Ah! Lettie, let me alone till your husband comes home, and then I'll leave all to him ; and if—"

" What !" exclaimed Lettie, giving her a shake, " let him, too, know I was a factory girl in England? Then," and she laughed bitterly, "my power over him would soon be gone, along with my pride before Mrs. Plantagenet. Ah! no; I'll be rid of you before that."

" So you are going to put me from your house?' said the mother, facing her.

" This moment, now, you old—"

" Before I go," shouted the mother, clutching her by the hair, "I say you *have* worked in a factory, and that I worked there to support you, and starved myself to do so."

Mrs. Phillips was mad. She knew Annie heard the shout, and, seizing her mother by the hair, dragged her to the door, and pushed her down the steps.

Annie and Kitty were nearly wild from fright. The desperate, unnatural act seemed to them like a dream.

Mrs. Phillips hastily closed the door and parlor-blinds, and rang for Annie.

" Tell her," said Kitty, "when you go up, that you are going to leave. Now, mind."

" Oh! yes, I shall," said Annie; "but I am afraid to venture near her."

" Go on," said the other; "I'll wait at the foot of the stairs here."

Annie, trembling, went up to the room, and, without giving her good mistress time to issue

any orders, told her she was going to leave im.
mediately, and hurried down again. Kitty assisted her in getting her articles ready, and both
set out for New York.

CHAPTER XXI.

O'ROURKE'S FORTUNES BEGIN TO IMPROVE.

HE journey to the little frame chapel amongst the Pennsylvania hills was so long and tedious that, travel as he would, James could never reach there before Mass had commenced, till at length the good pastor, Father Fitzsimons, noticing his bright, intelligent face and becoming manner in church, resolved to have a conversation with him, and from thenceforth service was delayed every Sunday morning till he would arrive.

Father Fitzsimons became a great friend to him, lending him books to read in the evenings, and allowing his father's letters to come in his care. This kindness from one whom he respected so much was a great consolation to James, and helped him to bear up against the hardships and privations of his position; for although he cared little for the toil of the fields, yet the wild and reckless class amongst whom he lived was a source of great pain to him.

During his first few weeks there, when the day's work was over, he would wander away

alone, and sit in some quiet spot where he might
not hear the curses, foul language, and drunken
shouts of the others, and think of Ireland, with its
quiet plains, gentle mountains and rivers, and green
hills with tall chapel-spires peeping over their tops
—an emblem of its people's devotion to God and
the Catholic Church. His mind would wander
away back to the time when Francis Reilly and
he used to carry little Annie to the school; to the
delight it caused when she clasped her tiny arms
around his neck as he lifted her over some dangerous part of the road, and with what caution
he used to watch lest Francis would deprive him
of the pleasure. Thus his memory would trace
every incident of their happy lives up to the last
evening by the river's bank. Then he would
vainly try to shut out the recollection of his
trials and fears since then, and hope that one day
Annie's face would smile on him again. But the
misery of his own present state, and the dread
of what may have befallen her, clouded the hope;
and, with as sad a heart as ever beat within a
breast, O'Rourke would return to his hut; and
so much did those bitter thoughts take hold of
his mind that he often lay insensible to shouts,
and uproar, and fighting around him. But when
he began to read the good books supplied him
by Father Fitzsimons, these gloomy thoughts

gradually brightened somewhat, and a new life seemed to open up before him.

Of all the men in the fields, he was the most attentive to his business, and never during the allotted hours for work idled away a moment. This, amongst so many who acted differently, could not escape the notice of the proprietor of the field. This latter, Mr. Lewis, was a very amiable, just, polite American gentleman, who always made it a rule to reward honesty and industry without regard to creed or nationality. It was his custom to make a round of his men thrice every day : shortly after they went to work in the morning, at noon, and again towards the close of the day. He was not a man to act on an impulse. Before taking a step, he waited and satisfied himself fully that it would not prove an injudicious one.

For some weeks after O'Rourke's arrival at the fields, Mr. Lewis, in his daily rounds, passed him by unnoticed. But by-and-by, James began to observe him letting his eye rest on him a little more than usual. At first he paid no attention to this, thinking probably the gentleman only remarked him as a stranger. One day, however, he was standing on the edge of the well, looking on at the work as usual, and the others were laboring with might and main for the time, when

James happened to raise his eyes in that direction, and saw Mr. Lewis regarding him very at-
tentively. James resumed his work, but, in a few
minutes, Mr. Lewis came over to him, and said :

"Young man, I wish to see you during the
evening ; don't be out of the road," and turned
away without giving the other time to speak.

Accordingly, when work was over, instead of
hiding himself from sight with his book, he waited
within view of the little wooden office, till Mr.
Lewis came to the door and beckoned him inside.
The gentleman was alone, and, returning to the
chair from which he had risen, crossed his legs as
James entered, and told him to sit down.

"Well, young man," were the first words, "how
do you like oil-digging?"

"Oh! I like the work very well, sir," was the
reply.

"Yes; but there is something else you don't
like quite so well," said the gentleman, with a
smile. "They are rough fellows, those diggers."

"I can get along with them very well, sir," said
James.

"Yes ; but don't you think you could get along
better at something else? You write a good
hand, do you?"

"I'll show you a specimen, if you please, sir,"
said James, greatly delighted.

"Well," said the other carelessly, drawing a sheet of paper from the drawer at his hand, and throwing it on the desk, "move your chair over here, and let me see what you can do. Just make a copy of that card." And he took one of his own from a large pocket-book on his knee.

James did so quickly and very neatly, handed it to Mr. Lewis, who, after one glance, put it in the pocket-book, and said:

"You write a very good hand indeed. Now what I want to propose to you is this: My business has increased so much of late, and I have so many men employed, that I cannot attend to all the duties of this office myself, and, if you think well of coming in here to assist me, I'll pay you a decent salary—something you can live on. Now, what do you say?"

No use in us saying what James said. He thanked his kind employer heartily, and, after receiving the keys of the office, retired with a joyous heart. Next morning found him seated in the office, dressed in his best clothes, busily engaged writing up and arranging the books, which want of time had compelled his employer to leave in a somewhat disordered way. He had everything in such good order that, when Mr. Lewis arrived and looked over his accounts, he smiled, and cast a look on James, as much as to say, "I have not mistaken my man this time, either," and walked out, as he said to himself, " Thank good- ness! that's so much off my mind."

Notwithstanding James differed so widely from the other workmen, and, as the saying is, " Made no freedom with any of them," they were delight- ed, one and all, at his good luck, and began at once to show him the respect he was now en- titled to, owing to the change in his position.

James did not take advantage of his newly-ac- quired power, as a great many in such cases usu- ally do, to win favor with his employer at the cost of the men. He became more sociable with them than had been his wont, and, now that his advice would be more heeded, used it trying to dissuade such of them as he imagined were not hopelessly lost to abandon drink and mend their lives in every way ; and it was far more delightful to him than the change in his own fortune, when, after a weary conversation, he induced our friend Dooley to come to church with him on Sunday.

CHAPTER XXII.

INTRODUCES A FASHIONABLE IRISH-AMERICAN LADY.

NNIE and her friend hastened as fast as they could to the nearest line of cars, and were soon across the ferry and riding up on the other side to Patrick Sweeny's. Mr. Sweeny and his wife were at home, and, when Kitty told them what had happened at the "mansion," they were greatly amused, and praised Annie's good sense for leaving such a place at once.

"Oh! yes," said Annie, "it were useless for me to think of living there any longer; they would frighten me to death. But the worst of it is, I am now idle."

"A very short time you need be," said Kitty. "You couldn't happen on a worse place anywhere than that."

"Why, bless you, Annie," said Mr. Sweeny, "what a greedy little thing you are! If ever anybody made a fortune in America, you will. The husband that gets you may take the world easy.'

All had a laugh at this, and after a few pleasant words all round Kitty went back to her place, and Annie into the little parlor to write a letter to her father and mother.

Mr. Sweeny would not hear of her advertising again, but promised to find her a suitable situation himself. This made Annie very happy, and the time was passing along nicely, till a tall, pale, smirking young lady of about twenty-five bounced into the parlor to spend the remainder of the evening. She wore a gray dress, very wide in the skirts, and very long and tight-fitting in the body, with two closely-planted rows of bright buttons in front, like those on a huzzar's jacket, a white hat drawn over her eyes, and carried in her hand an immense fan, which she continued to wave desperately. That she was not much of a favorite with the family was evident to Annie from the manner of her reception. Mrs. Sweeny, without rising from her seat, merely said, "Good-evening, Miss Talbot;" and Sweeny did not seem to notice her at all.

"Well! well! I do declare," said she, dropping into a chair, "the heat and closeness of this place take the breath from me. Whew! goodness gracious me!"

"'Tis very warm out this evening," said Mrs. Sweeny, raising the window a little, "and, insi...

of being so very hot here, I always find a nice draught in this room."

Miss Talbot made no reply, but leaned her head a little one side, and fanned away. Sweeny and his wife exchanged looks, and the former, with an expression of disgust on his face, rose and went outside on the stoop.

"I'm pretty well used up," said the charming damsel at length languidly, and letting the fan drop. "I was up the road to-day, and what a charming prospect, I do declare!"

"Oh! you were out carriage-riding," said Mrs. Sweeny, with a slight smile.

"*We* call it going up the road, and not carriage-riding any more," said Miss Talbot emphatically. "That word 'carriage-riding'"—this with scorn— "is in everybody's mouth now; so, of course, *we* had to go to work and give it a name that we'd com-*pre*-hend amongst ourselves. You didn't go, as intended, to the country this summer, eh?"

"Only for a day or two," said Mrs. Sweeny.

Miss Talbot, with a sudden start, picked up her fan, and, wheeling herself around, looked closely into Annie's face, while she hummed a lively air. The poor girl blushed deeply, and, rising, went to another part of the room, Miss Talbot's eyes in quick pursuit. "From Ireland, I'll bet a dollar, come," said she, turning her eyes on Mrs. Sweeny.

" Yes; the lady is just as much Irish as you are yourself," said that lady. " It should not require much penetration on your part to tell that."

"*Me* Irish!" said she, with a short nod of great force. " *I* am no such a thing. Is it because father and mother was rose there that *I* am Irish ?"

" Exactly; there could be no better reason," said Mrs. Sweeny.

Miss Talbot stood up as if to depart, which would have been a great calamity just then ; but after twisting her face a few times like a short-sighted man with a bad razor, she went to the window, and began beating a tune with her fingers on the glass. Annie and Miss Sweeny had a hard task to restrain their laughter.

" Please don't rap the window that way," said Mrs. Sweeny, a little sharply, " you will attract the attention of the people outside. See, there is a butcher on the far side thinks you're calling him."

" You wouldn't have received this visitation this evening at all," said the indignant lady, " only Mr. La Bunty is off to Chicago, and Mr. Delblether's niece has the cholera-morbus after all the mushmelons she ate at Coney Island last Sunday. There *wus* three doctors and two nurses up with her night and day since."

Mrs. Sweeny expressed her great sorrow for the critical condition of the young lady, and asked how she had been so unfortunate as to imperil her life in such a way.

"Oh! Mr. Frank Driggler was telling me all about it," said she, again sitting down and clasping her hands. "I went up the road with him to-day, just because the other gentlemen were engaged. Well, you know Mr. Delblether, and old Mrs. Delblether, and Miss Delblether went to Coney Island last Sunday. They went down on their knees to me to go; but, stuff!" And she tossed her head. "When they got there, who does they meet but Mrs. Cyrus Xersus Smot and her daughter, that came home from the boarding-school only a few weeks ago. Well, Mrs. Smot, you know, thinks there's not the like of her daughter in the world; so she thought she'd show off a little, and put on airs. They weren't two minutes talking, till she began to boast of her daughter's accomplishments, and how beautiful and healthy she was. Mrs. Delblether made up her mind to not let her have it all her own way; so she says, says Mrs. Delblether, ' My granddaughter here knows more than could be pounded into your daughter's head in forty thousand years. Talk of your daughter's beauty, and her shoulders not the breadth of my hand. Talk of her health. Why my granddaughter wasn't a day sick in eleven years, when she had the shakes, and your daughter was home two weeks lying with you last fall. And speak of accomplishments: my granddaughter knows how to eat like a Christian, and has the best appetite of any young lady in New York. I would put her for fifty dollars against yours, starved and thin as she is, coming from that hungry school.' 'I'll take your bet,' says Mrs. Smot, pulling out her purse. She has plenty of stamps, no getting out of that. 'It's done,' says Mrs. Delblether, covering the money in a gentleman's hand—a mutual friend. 'My dear Bella, an't you in tune for a good feed after so much sea air, and the credit of our family at stake?' says Mrs. Delblether. 'Rely on me, grandma,' says Bella, opening her stays. 'What's the thing going to be?' 'Mushmelons,' shouted Mrs. Smot. You know they lived in Georgia one time, and were used to melons. 'That's not square,' says Mrs. Delblether. 'Never mind, grandma, I'll go it,' says Bella. 'Let it be mushmelons.'

"The mutual friend hailed a vender, and told him to drive round behind a sandbank. He did so, and the wagon-load was purchased, and the young ladies pitched in. Well, to make a long story short, Bella was eating away, nothing the worse,

only her eyes rolling a little, when Miss Smot
gave a terrible roar, and fell back in a faint in
her mother's arms. They had the same number
eaten at this time; but Bella never ceased till
she finished three more. Her grandma begged
her, with tears in her eyes, to make it five; but
the brave girl didn't feel as if she could. Miss
Smot was carried away by four men, in her
mother's shawl, but Bella was able to walk, with
the assistance of her uncle and grandmother, to
the boat; and, when the excited crowd began to
cheer, she begged to be left to herself, and walked
ten yards without a hand to her. Coming home
on the boat, she drank a quantity of apple-sauce,
and, if it hadn't been for that, she'd have been on
her feet in two days. But she took on terrible
that night; a-yelling and a-twisting herself so
that they thought she was gone, sure pop. She
is not much better yet; but her grandma is so
proud of her that she'll spare no cost to bring
her round. And why should she? See how ad-
mired Bella 'll be now in society." And Miss
Talbot finished with a sigh, as if she wished she
could do something to gain renown.

Annie thought the story a great joke; but, on
being told by Miss Sweeny it was every word true,
she laughed till the tears rolled down her cheeks.
Mrs. Sweeny was well used to such entertaining

accounts of high life from Miss Talbot, and made no remark on the thrilling contest; but, after a pause, asked her when she intended fulfilling her promise to visit Europe.

" Not this season; 'tis too late now," she replied carelessly.

" Then next summer?" said the other.

" Oh! I rather guess I shall," was the reply. " And when I come to say good-by, 'tis not Miss Talbot you'll see, I reckon."

" Oh! 'twill be Mrs. Delblether we'll have then," said Mrs. Sweeny, with a smile.

" Yes," said she carelessly, " the thing is to come off during the holidays."

" I suppose, much as you dislike Ireland, you'll not omit paying it a visit," said Mrs. Sweeny.

" I guess I'll make a call there. For my part, I don't care; but Mr. Delblether says we shall. He thinks 'twill be so very amusing. But I have my fears for him; he's such a man to laugh that he may kill himself when he goes there."

" Kitty is thinking of paying a visit to her mother next year," said Annie, addressing Mrs. Sweeny.

" Indeed, then," put in Miss Talbot, before the person spoken to had time to answer, " I'll call on Kitty if we're in Ireland together, and see what them little villages with the noisy boys and girls look like. I'll bet they keep pretty mum while we're there."

"Yes," said Annie, with an arch smile. "I dare say you'll surprise them somewhat. It's not very often they see such an extraordinary lady as you."

" Never you mind," said the other, " if we don't make them stare! Are there any gentlemen or ladies, or is there any society at all in Ireland?" she asked, after a pause.

" A few," said Mrs. Sweeny.

"Oh! then, I suppose they'll bother the life out of us so much with invitations that we won't know what to do."

" I don't think you have much to dread in that way," said Annie.

" I'll not put up with it; that's how I'll fix the thing," said she. " If I think any of them worth visiting, why, all right."

A long pause followed, which was broken by Mr. Sweeny returning to the parlor, and expressing his surprise at the lateness of the hour. The young lady, however, did not take the hint, but fiercely assailed him with questions on different public matters, not one of which she allowed him to answer; gave her own views and the opinions of numerous intellectual acquaintances of hers, stood up, went to the door, came back again, till the family were in a state of distraction.   At last she went outside, still talking, and Mr. Sweeny, who was standing in the hall listening to her, hastily closed the door.

" What a strange character she is !" said Annie. " I hope there are few American ladies like Mrs. Phillips and her."

" No American ladies at all like either of them or their acquaintances," said Mrs. Sweeny. " She belongs to a class—and a very large class, too, in this city—who think they'll be more thought of by the American people for denying their country and often their religion.   Now, for my part, I don't see how they can be so short-sighted ; because, of all the people in the world, none despise the mean and false-hearted more than the Americans."

CHAPTER XXIII.

KITTY BRADY REVISITS THE OLD LAND, AND IS VISITED BY THE FASHIONABLE IRISH-AMERICAN LADY.

R. SWEENY procured Annie a situation in a very respectable family, whose home was on the banks of the Hudson, where she lived contentedly till an event occurred, of which we shall speak further on, which greatly changed the course of her life.

Our story now moves on one year, and we find Kitty Brady standing on the quay, waiting to go aboard a ship which is about to sail for Queenstown. Annie, Mrs. Sweeny, her husband and daughter, and Francis Reilly are standing around her. Francis had arrived a few months before, and carried such an earnest request to Kitty to visit her mother in the old land that it put an end to her wavering on that point. Kitty is much affected at parting from her friends, and her tears are falling fast. They are talking of the great happiness before her, to visit again the scenes of her childhood, and once more hear the only voice that sustained her there. Her trunk, which has been taken aboard, is filled with presents, neat and tasteful, sent by Annie and her brother to their parents at home.

The moment for parting comes; all bid her an affectionate good-by, and pray a blessing on her journey.

Kitty had sent a letter apprising her mother of the day she intended leaving New York. Mrs. Brady hastened to Farrell Reilly's, told them the joyful news, and insisted on their coming to the cabin the day her daughter was expected to arrive. Mrs. Reilly and her husband were greatly delighted at the prospect of speaking to one who had so lately seen their children, and promised the old woman they would be with her on that day.

Mrs. Brady could not wait patiently till the arrival of the happy day. She walked along the road in the direction of the railway station, first by the broad road, and then by the narrow lane which ran across the hills, dreading, if she travelled one way only, Kitty might be coming by the other; climbed up with great toil, which she felt not, to the top of the steep hill which overhung the cabin, and looked along the river-bank in every direction. Then, after all this hardship, she would recollect Kitty had not time to reach

any of those places yet; so she would return to
the cabin, and weep and pray till another morning came. At length—and it seemed to her she
had been watching for it a year—the day, about
which there could be no mistake, arrived, and
Farrell and his wife were early in the cabin—so
early that the first rays of the rising sun were
barely visible on the tops of the tallest trees.
Already Mrs. Brady was standing outside the
door waiting for them.

"O Farrell! I am afraid of my life we will
be too late. Do you think we will, Mrs. Reilly?"
said she, turning from one to the other. "It
seems an age since daylight."

"We shall be early enough, Nancy," said Farrell, following his wife into the cabin. "The train
from Cork will not arrive for two hours yet, and
Mrs. Reilly is very tired, so I think we may rest
a little."

"Surely, poor dear, she is tired," said Nancy,
hastily handing her the best chair in the cabin.
"And now, Farrell, while you and her rest yourselves, I'll just run as far as the brae, and see if
there's any sight of her. The train may come
early this morning."

"I wish it may," said Farrell; "but there is
little use in your expecting that. Better give

yourself as little fatigue as you can; you will want all your strength when Kitty comes."

"Oh! I feel as lively these days, Farrell," said she, "as I did thirty years ago. Two hours is such a terrible wait. No harm in me trying, anyway."

"We'll go with you very soon, Nancy," said Mrs. Reilly. "We can walk along leisurely."

Nancy insisted no further, but went out on the lane, and returned with word that the cattle were rising from their resting-places and beginning to feed, and that "Pat the Brock," the apple-man, had just passed by on his way to town.

"And look," she added, lifting an old tin lid from a crevice in the wall, and letting in a tiny stream of sunlight, "the sun does not come in here till very late."

Farrell and his wife could not dispute those convincing evidences of the lateness of the hour, and stood up to accompany her to the station. When they reached there, the depot looked the most deserted of any building they had passed. An odd, smoke-begrimed car stood on the track here and there, looking as if they had made up their minds to travel no more, and were very sorry for travelling so much.

The doors were closed, and no one to be seen except a large, lazy-looking porter in his black

corduroys, and smoky hair enough on his head
for ten porters, walking slowly along, the echo
of his heavy footfall only adding to the loneliness
of the situation.

Mrs. Brady and her friends sat down on a
large wooden box at one end of the building, to
wait. By-and-by the doors began slowly to open
—so slow that they seemed in doubt whether to
close again or not—and a few more porters appeared, all differing so much in everything except
corduroy that any one not in the secret would
think they were born at least a thousand miles
apart. Soon a guard showed himself in brass
buttons and a yellow band around his cap, looking so very important, disdainful, and impolite
that passengers under his care must have looked
on themselves as in a jail for the time being.

A little later, and an occasional traveller wandered into the building; one now, then another,
then three or four together, till the place became
lively with people. Commercial travellers, with
immense light bags in their hands and short lead-
pencils behind their ears, walked to and fro; large,
fat, good-humored-looking farmers leaned against
the pillars, and discussed the markets; keen-eyed
stylishly-clad gentlemen, some old, others young,
and all carrying large umbrellas, bustled in and
out of the crowds, not together, but separately.

as if they were engaged to count the number of
people around, and were determined, at all costs,
to do so correctly. It seemed remarkable, the
deference shown these gentlemen by every one
present, especially the farmers, who gave each
berth wide enough for a coach and four, and
muttered as he passed, "Damn those attor-
neys!"

At length the ticket-office was opened, and
all gathered around the little window, crushing,
scrambling, and scolding ; for the train which was
to bear them away was moving into the depot.
When about half the passengers had received
tickets, the train began to move off again, and
the uproar at the office became deafening. The
nimble clerk, however, supplied these latter in
time to get aboard after an exciting race, and the
building settled into another half hour's repose.

As the time for the arrival of their train approached, Farrell and his companions were in a
fever of anxiety. Mrs. Brady asked every porter
she saw at least ten times what the exact minute would be. They were standing together at
the south end of the depot, looking along the
track, when a cloud of smoke rose over the low hill
near by, and the station bell began to ring loudly.

"Here it is at last!" exclaimed Farrell.

"Oh! thank heaven," said Nancy, clasping Mrs.

Reilly by the hand in her joyous excitement.
"Oh! God be praised that I have lived to see
this day."

The three stood, their eyes fixed on the long
line of coaches gliding up. The train soon
stopped, and every window was filled with eager
faces looking out on those on the platform, and
the doors crowded with men, women, bundles,
bags, and children hurrying down on the flags.
Farrell and the two women ran wildly from window to window, from door to door, eagerly scanning each female face. But the cars were empty,
and the crowd beginning to disperse, and they
had seen no sign of Kitty.

Poor Nancy's heart sank, and a mist stood before her and those around. Neither of her companions ventured to speak what they thought.

"O my child!" said the distracted woman
faintly, "if she is not here—"

"Hush a moment!" exclaimed Farrell. "There
is a young woman dressed in green with her back
to us, standing by the trunk down there—"

But before he could finish the sentence, the
young lady turned and looked towards them, and
with a cry of joy ran up, and mother and daughter were folded in each other's arms. Poor
Nancy was wild with delight. Her tears fell on
the face, neck, and hands of her child. Again

and again she kissed her frantically, and breathed blessings on her, till Mrs. Reilly said :

" Nancy, you must not think of keeping her all to yourself; let me kiss and welcome the darling girl."

The old woman said, her face against her daughter's :

" Kitty, my loving child, Mrs. Reilly is here to meet you, too, and her husband. Every one must be glad to see you."

The greeting between Mrs. Reilly and the girl was hardly less warm, and, after embracing Far-rell, and answering numerous questions about her-self and his children, the happy little party set out for the cabin.

The number of callers on Kitty, every one of whom were delighted with her handsome appear-ance and nice manners, was immense. Poor Nancy was almost wild with joy. The good, truthful account she gave of Francis and Annie made their parents very happy, and, for the first time during its existence, Nancy Brady's cabin was the scene of contentment and happiness. Time, which heretofore hung so heavily on Nancy's hands, swept past quickly now. Every day brought some new enjoyment ; some old place of historic interest, about which Kitty had read in America, was to be visited ; some far-off

neighbor, whose friend or friends had sent mes-
sages to those at home, were to be seen; and, as
she always insisted on her mother accompanying
her, Nancy saw more strange places and people,
and learned more of Ireland's story the first
month her daughter spent at home, than she had
during her previous life. Invitations from old
and new acquaintances were numerous, and even
Father Fitzpatrick called one day and took both
to his house to spend the evening; and, finding
Kitty so well informed and so intelligent, many a
chat they had together during the summer. Mrs.
Reilly let no day pass without seeing her, and
often they went down together by the river's
bank, and sat talking, till Nancy, who would insist
on staying behind to prepare a feast, would have
to go in search of them.

On one of these occasions, the old woman had
just thrown her shawl about her shoulders to sally
out in search of the "pair," as she called them,
when, happening to look through the little window,
she saw a very stylishly-dressed gentleman and
lady standing outside, the former pointing with
his cane towards the door, and the latter, with her
hand pressed against her side, laughing heartily

This sudden sight alarmed the old woman somewhat, and she hesitated a moment, in hopes they
might pass on. But to her horror, after apparent-

ly satisfying themselves by scrutinizing the cabin, both came over to the door, and the lady enquired, in a voice which sounded so high up in her nose that Nancy thought she must be suffering from a severe cold, if that was where Kitty Brady lived.

"Oh! yes, yes; please sit down a moment," said the old woman, handing each a chair. "I'll call her directly."

The lady declined the proffered accommodation with a wave of her hand, and the gentleman went over and looked into the little room, the door of which was open, and began to whistle softly. Nancy looked from one to the other in amazement, not rightly knowing what to do.

"Oh! hurry up, and tell her right away, will you?" said the lady, after she had swept the floor with her skirt a few times. Nancy hastened as fast as she could to the river's bank, and told Kitty in such an excited manner that two very odd-looking people were waiting in the house to see her that she hurried in as quick as she could, and left her mother and Mrs. Reilly to follow after

CHAPTER XXIV.

EXPERIENCES OF THE FASHIONABLE LADY AND
HER HUSBAND IN IRELAND.—ENTERTAINING
THE GUESTS AT A HOTEL.—A LECTURE IN A
FORGE, AND WHAT CAME OF IT.

HE "odd-looking" pair who had caused
Nancy so much alarm were a no less
couple than Mr. Delblether and his
wife, the once charming Miss Talbot
" The thing *did* come off during the holidays,'
and they were now on a pleasure trip to Europe.

To say Kitty was delighted to see them might
be venturing on an assertion not strictly true; but
she gave them a kindly welcome, and offered the
hospitalities of her mother's cottage, which was
rejected by Mrs. Delblether, who declared, with
a frown and shake of her head, that to swallow
anything under such a low roof would surely choke
her. Kitty thought of the dreadful misfortune
this would entail on so many, and pressed her no
further. The husband, however, drank a large
glassful of pure usquebaugh, and, declaring that
he was something very low and mean if he didn't
like it exceedingly, finished another. As Kitty or

her companions did not like to lead the conversation when two such distinguished people were present, and as the distinguished people did not show much inclination to talk, a very awkward half-hour was spent, at the end of which Mrs. Delblether said :

"Kitty, me and Mr. Delblether wishes to take a look around this location at the *fowling* and *shooting*, and so on ; so we've put up at that place you call a hotel in the village, and we want you to pay us a visit there."

Kitty promised to do so, and the visitors walked away, each looking peculiarly and unaccountably sad.

Now, as our restless thoughts can travel much quicker than Kitty's feet, we will precede her, and see how her exalted friends are getting on in the village alone.

They arrived at the hotel early in the evening, and spent the time till supper in their own apartments, planning the measures they would adopt to let the quiet villagers know they were something the like of which probably had never honored them with a visit before.

Mrs. Delblether was by far the better strategist. Her plans were numerous and well laid, while all her husband could think of was for him to put a long cigar in his mouth, with his hat greatly on one side, his wife to hang her gold watch around her neck, and let it fall down exposed to view on her breast.

She derided his want of tact, and commanded his attention to listen to *her*.

" Now, you see," she said, "it's all very good to stagger them in the hotel here ; but something must be done outside, otherwise half the people may never hear of us at all. To do the thing square inside here you may rely on me, and when we are out together, too. But you know there are some places where you can do a good deal if you only have the pluck. Now, when we were coming up-stairs, you remember me stopping behind for a little ?" He did not forget it. " Well, there were two men talking in the room on the right, and laughing very heartily over something that had happened in the forge. One of them said, ' I heard the words plainly, and more than twenty men standing around at the time.' Now, anywhere in such a small ranch as this, where twenty men can be found together must be the chief place of resort, eh ?" He held the same opinion. " So I want you to go there to-morrow evening, and just begin by comparing *everything* you have seen in Ireland with *everything* in America. Tell them they hain't nothin' here like New York. Tell them they're darn fools for living in such a country at all, and even go so far as to despise the forge and blacksmith, too."

The gentleman was delighted, and declared he surely would have thought of this himself before morning; whereupon the lady said he would not, and went so far as to say she never knew him to think of anything he should. Soon after, they descended to the dining-room.

A number of jovial-looking men, some standing by the windows, others seated at the board, were in the room.

Mrs. Delblether seated herself with a loud "Oh!" as if the act distressed her, sat up very erect, and, gathering her eyebrows into an expression of keen scrutiny, looked from face to face, down one side of the table, then up the other. Her husband took his place by her side, and closed his eyes so as to leave only the pupil visible, and resting an arm on the table, threw the other over the back of his chair, and waited for his accomplished wife to commence. When she had satisfied herself looking at the live faces, she turned her attention to the painted ones on the wall, and, singling out a portrait of O'Connell which hung over the chimney-piece, asked, as she pointed her knife in that direction, and looked at a gentleman opposite, "Whose is that? Tell me, will you?"

He hastily informed her, and she said, letting her head fall back, " Mr. Delblether, that's who the Irish in New York talk so much about. Well, only think; no nice paintings even to be seen in this 'ere—I don't 'zactly know what to call it."

The guests, who up to this had managed to preserve their decorum, all glanced at her, and a smile overspread every face.

She kept silent for a moment, eating away rapidly, her face almost on the plate, then leaned over and whispered in her husband's ear, " Why don't you say something? You look as glum as a pumpkin."

" You're a-staggering them yourself. Go on, I am proud of you," whispered he in return. " Leave me toe to-morrow evening."

And she did go on, asking questions about this article and that; what the table was made of, how much it cost; how much difference in the price of the black-handled knives and the white ones; were dishes and salt-cellars sold on time, and, if so, how much discount was allowed for cash payment; and even went so far as to ask an old gentleman at the lower end of the table how long after he purchased his wig did the maker wait till he sent in his bill. On every reply to those questions, she commented at moderate length, and drew numerous parallels between Ireland and America, to the great disadvantage of the former.

Soon the guests began to perceive they had found a treasure, and employed every means to make the most of it. All heartily coincided with her remarks, and outwardly thanked Providence for sending such an enlightened angel to tell them of their failings, and point out to them so many remedies. Not one of them, except those whom pressing duty called away, left the hotel that night, and even those latter lingered till the last second, and looked back regretfully as they went from the room.

Mrs. Delblether talked till after midnight. There was such a crowd at the breakfast-table the following morning that the landlord, in his hurry and excitement, broke a pitcher over a slow waiter's head, and pushed another from the kitchen with such force that he fell on the tray he was carrying with a terrible noise, crushing its contents. One maid inflicted a severe wound on the palm of her hand with a carving-fork, and another fell headlong into the coal-cellar. That evening, Mr. Delblether, dressed in a long black coat of very cheap material, tight-fitting, short, check pants, a soft, wide-brimmed hat, and a cigar in his mouth, sauntered up the street to the forge, to commence his grand attack on the attention of the villagers. The blacksmith, a big, hearty-looking fellow, with a laugh ringing as his anvil, kindly saluted him as he entered. A number of men and boys were in the forge at the time, sitting up on the hearth or standing about the floor, amongst whom he noticed many of those he had seen at the hotel.

He returned the smith's friendly nod with another of quiet patronage, and, closing one eye, took a deliberate survey of those present—the walls, the roof, and behind the bellows. During this time, he had not spoken a word, but hummed merrily.

" Say, young fellar," said he at length, balancing himself on his cane, and looking at the blacksmith, " how do the farmers cultivate the sile in these 'ere diggins?"

" They have a number of ways, sir," said the man addressed.

" Everything is done by system, sir, in my country, and done co-rectly. We hain't no two ways of doing anything, we haven't," said he.

" None but the right way?" said the smith, with a smile.

" The right way or no way, sir," said the gentleman, shaking his watch-chain, " that's our motto.'

" I suppose you find things very different here

from your own country," said a man, coming forward and resting his foot on the side of the trough.

"Etarnally so," was the reply. "Why, hold on, me friend. If I ever seed anything to come up to the difference between America and this little island, I am— Why, sir, in the first place, I could find you a squash-field in Jarsey bigger than your whole country. And, again, you have no leading questions that I'd bother with. Look at our tar-and-feather compromise question in the West; why, it's ahead of—of— everything," said he, unable to find a better expression. "Then our rivers—what are ye talking about? Why, one on 'em would flow square round your country ten times. Think of our mountains, and snakes, and muskiters; why, you have nothing here." And he moved his head from side to side in disgust.

Those in the forge gathered closely around, hardly giving him room to swing his coat-tails in, and the blacksmith rested on his sledge, and looked on entranced. Others outside, hearing by some means of what was going on, came crowding in, till the little place was filled to overflowing. The door was packed, and even the little window had its two or three rows of heads. Still they kept coming; men in every variety of dress; women, some with shawls about their shoulders, others with children in their arms hastily snatched from their cradles; boys with books in their hands, from which they had been studying to-morrow's lessons: and even little creatures not long out of their swaddling-clothes were met making their way along the street, and, when questioned as to their destination, looked up and lisped, " The yantee," and ran on. Dogs, seeing they had the place to themselves, worried each other behind the houses, and pursued stray cats and pigs along the street. Philosophic old cocks who had lived all their lives in the village stretched their necks and tried to think; but, arriving at no satisfactory conclusion, fluttered across the wall into the chapel-yard, and frantically called on their charge to follow them. Never was such uproar and confusion witnessed in the town before.

Mr. Delblether was delighted. He could hear those in the rear of the crowd exclaiming, " Where is he? Why don't they put him up on the hearth, and give us all a chance to see him?" A chance was offered him to " come out strong," and probably to make himself famous. So letting his tongue and arms loose, he commenced a harangue on the disadvantages under which he claimed the village and, in fact, all Ireland labored: be-

sought his hearers to learn something from the
example set them by New York, with its theatres,
parks, savings-banks, and steamboats; told them,
if he had their village in America, he would bore
a canal to the ocean, and have all those institutions flourishing in it before three months.

The audience fairly danced with joy. Since
Bell's circus visited them, thirteen years before,
they had not had such amusement. The worthy
entertainer was asked numerous questions, to
which he made prompt replies; asked himself
several, and answered them as cleverly; skipped
admirably from one topic to another; confounded
names, dates, and facts delightfully; was sarcastic
at one time, pathetic at another, and frequently
very humorous. He spoke every word with such
a genuine twang that not a few on the edge of
the crowd cursed whoever was "dinging" the
anvil.

How long he might have continued it is hard
to say, had he not been somewhat rudely silenced
by a prolonged clanging noise outside, followed
by a loud, mirthful cheer. He looked wildly at
the blacksmith, and asked what the uproar meant.

"That's the way," replied that gentleman
with great politeness (for a blacksmith), "they
have of honoring celebrated personages like yourself."

"Oh! by Jove," thought Mr. Delblether, ' they are going to serenade me ; but," he added aloud, " your music is very coarse."

He turned to look around on his hearers before resuming his discourse, but found the greater part of them had gone into the street, and what remained were huddled together at the lower end of the forge, like men seeking shelter from a shower. Thoroughly surprised now, he was about to make some remark ; but, before he could do so, the candle disappeared from its place, leaving the shop in total darkness, and a heavy thud sounded along the roof, which caused him to look up in terror and in time to have his eyes, nose, and mouth filled with dust. He ran towards the door, but a well-directed stream of water from the trough covered him from head to foot before he gained the street. Blind with dust and rage, he knew not what direction to take, but stood rubbing his blackened hands to his blacker face, till a motley crowd of boys, with old tin cans, broken kettles, scraps of iron, and, in short, everything convenient that could make a noise, formed a ring around him. At a signal from the leader, they struck up such a horrible, deafening r—r—r—rip that the recipient of the honor fairly jumped from the ground. In vain he tried to make his voice heard ; but the

more excited he became, the more his tormentors
banged their *instruments.*

At length they parted on one side to let him
out, which, when he saw, he dashed from their
midst down the street towards' his hotel like a
madman.   They allowed him to gain a little on
them, so as to give effect to the thing, and then
started in pursuit with even greater uproar, followed by the dogs, which had by this time grown
reckless. and boldly ran into the street, barking
furiously. Boys heretofore timid in their excitement wrenched old lids from others whom they
dreaded up to that night. Grown-up lads threw
down their smaller companions, and dragged
them along the pavement till they surrendered
whatever engine of noise they carried.   Some,
who could find nothing else, tore up paving-
stones, and, holding one in each hand, rapped
them together as they ran.   Mr. Delblether
having reached the hotel, the serenaders gathered around the door, cheered, yelled, laughed,
rapped their cans a few times. and then disappeared as suddenly as they came. Mrs. Delblether screamed loud and regularly for ten
minutes after her husband's arrival. He was
blacker than any charcoal nigger she had ever
seen and the dust filled his mouth so that he
could not speak. At length, when his face re-

sumed its natural color somewhat, which it did
after blacking all the water in the room, and five
or six jugfuls carried up by a waiter, she recovered sufficiently to ask what had befallen him;
and when he told her, she attributed the whole
misfortune to his own awkwardness, and " wa-
gered," if she had been in his place, the story
would be a different one.

They left town a few days afterwards, and Mr.
Lacy was the only inhabitant who regretted their
ever coming there. For two months after their
departure, he broke more rods on boys than he
had in as many years before. They neglected
their books, and took to drawing likenesses of Mr.
Delblether as he appeared addressing the crowd
in the forge on that eventful night, and as he
looked flying down the street during the serenade.

CHAPTER XXV.

ANNIE AND JAMES HAPPY.

GAIN our tale moves on, this time to the end. A few years have passed by, and Annie yet lives with the good, kind family on the banks of the Hudson. Francis is in good employment in New York City, Patrick Sweeny and his small family live in the same quiet happiness, and Kitty Brady is married to the young man who put such an abrupt end to the Scotchman's love for Annie.

It is a bright, pleasant Sunday morning in April, with a gentle breeze waving the white curtains on the raised windows, that Kitty and her husband are standing together in the neat little room, both dressed for church. Mrs. Ryan, for that is Kitty's name now, has been to the window half a dozen times, peeping into the street below.

"I wonder what can be keeping her," she says at length. "I thought she'd have been here an hour ago."

Mr. Ryan looks at his watch, and says ·

"They have twenty minutes yet."

"Oh! but think of the journey to Barclay Street—"

She had not finished the sentence, when the door was pushed open, and Annie walked into the room.

" I thought you would never come, my Annie," said Mrs. Ryan, kissing her fondly, "My eyes are tired watching for you."

"Oh !" said Annie, giving her hand to Mr. Ryan, " I couldn't help it, Kitty. The train was delayed an hour this morning."

Notwithstanding her hurry a few minutes before, Mrs. Ryan sat down, and began asking the girl numerous questions as to how she had spent the time since she saw her last, and compliment her on how well and handsome she looked, till her husband said, with a smile :

" Ladies, I think you had better come on now. You will have time enough for the like of that during the evening."

The three then hurried out and into a car, and in a short time reached Barclay Street, where they alighted, and entered St. Peter's Church just as High Mass commenced. The church was very crowded, but two gentlemen resigned their seats to Annie and Mrs. Ryan, one of whom moved up towards the altar, and the other knelt down by Ryan's side in the passage.

Had Annie's eyes been raised as the latter gentleman passed by her, she would have noticed the surprised look with which he regarded her.

The music of the grand organ filled the building, and mounted up heavenwards, carrying with it the homage and adoration of the kneeling multitude; and Annie bowed her head low in earnest prayer, and was soon lost to every thought of earth. The gentleman knelt at the end of her seat, and, when Ryan happened to raise his eyes in that direction, he could see him glance at the devout girl with a strange, wild look, then turn his face towards the altar, and pray fervently. Of this, however, Ryan took no notice, till, during the sermon, he could not help remarking the strange manner of the man, who seemed to be acting in a way which he himself could not control. His face was suffused with blushes. He knew the people near by could not avoid noticing him, but still he looked at Annie with a restless gaze, his lips moving as if to speak, and his feet rubbing the floor nervously. It seemed that, if she turned her face towards him, he would lose his senses, and spring to her side at once. But Annie's eyes were cast down, and she was utterly unconscious of the anxious, agitated face watching her. Was one of those gentle prayers breathed for the welfare of its owner?

We know Annie was not unmindful of the promise she made that evening long ago, with none
but the moon and stars for her witness.

At length, the ceremony over, the people began to leave the church. The greater part of
the congregation, however, had departed, and
the altar-lights were extinguished when Annie
and Mrs. Ryan rose to leave; the gentleman
stood up from his knees at the same moment,
and, if Annie felt a hand gently, very gently
touch hers, she did not notice it, but went down
the aisle with her two companions, followed by
the stranger; they were about to descend the
steps, when a voice behind her said, "Annie!"
She turned around, but seeing it was a young gentleman whom she did not know that addressed
her, and thinking he mistook her for some other
person, turned away quickly, and had reached the
sidewalk, when he came to her side, and, looking
into her face, said mournfully:

"Annie, don't you know me? I would have
known you at the end of fifty years."

She looked at him in surprise. A strange, un-
explainable feeling came over her; tears started
to her eyes, and her limbs grew weak. James
O'Rourke came into her mind, probably because
the thought of him was uppermost there. But,
no; the richly-clad, wealthy-looking gentleman

by her side could not be he. Nonsense! Poor James, who ran away from her that night on the river's bank with worn, patched clothes, and barely sufficient to bring him to America in his pocket!

"I do not know you, sir," she replied, in a low, broken voice, and tried to move on.

But he caught her by the hand, and exclaimed, "Oh! yes, you do, Annie; don't say you forget your own James."

Poor Annie fell against his shoulder. "Oh! heavens, James, and this really is yourself," she murmured through her tears.

He drew her closer to his heart, and said, "Oh! yes, yes, Annie, my love, it is I at last."

"O James! how I have watched and prayed for this meeting these long years!" sobbed the girl.

"Not more earnestly, at least, than I have, Annie. The thought of you, my dearest, has not left my mind an hour, day or night, since that misty evening. It surely was the good God, who has watched over us both during those weary years, sent me here to-day. I knew your sweet face the moment I saw you in church, and it nearly drove me wild that I could not make myself known on the spot."

"Ah! little I thought," said Annie, "when my

mind was so full of you leaving the chapel—for I can never look on a crowd of people but some one amongst them reminds me of you—that at that moment you were so near."

"Now, Annie," said he, "all our misery and anxiety are melted away, and we shall not run the risk of their returning again by parting any more."

Mr. Ryan and his wife being introduced, James was greatly delighted to see the latter, and learn how well she had done.

"I will not ask you, Annie, how you have got through this time ; it is sufficient for me to see you are alive and well. Oh! what dreadful misgivings I had when every effort to find you failed! One time I thought my dear Annie might have died on the voyage ; and again, that, lone and friendless in America, she broke her little heart."

Mr. Ryan invited him to accompany them to his house for the evening. James readily agreed, and, hastily telling a fellow-guest at a hotel near by, who had accompanied him to church, that he would be absent for the evening, hailed a carriage, and they were soon in the little, airy room, with Mrs. Ryan bustling here and there preparing dinner.

What a change had come over Annie's life since she left that little room in the morning! Then

she was not very unhappy, but the painful sense
of something wanting, which distressed her so
often during those years, was now banished
Now her heart was full, overflowing with joy,
and the tears which the " little lion " could keep
back in the presence of misfortune and grief fell
freely now that she was supremely happy. James
had been a good, religious man she could tell
during his long absence. from her sight. No
crime or vice had set their mark on his countenance. It was as bright, genial, and intellectual
as when she gazed on it unawares as he played
or sang for her on the green hill-top. His upright life was receiving its reward even here. He
was on the high-road to fortune, if he had not
already reached its golden gates. His employer,
in return for his industry and ability, had made
him a partner with himself. And what shall we
say of his happiness now? All the fears that
embittered his life so long at an end ; the dream
of years fulfilled ; Annie, whose shadow he traced
in the twilight, whose smile the moonbeams re-
flected, was now by his side, more beautiful than
his imagination had ever painted her, never to
leave him again. Yes, Annie and James were
very, very happy that Sunday evening in Kitty's
little parlor.

By-and-by Francis called to see his sister, and

the meeting between the two schoolmates was very cordial. Mr. Sweeny and his wife and daughter dropped in during the evening, and every one felt in such excellent spirits that a happier little party never were together. Mr. Sweeny had a joke on every one. Even Annie came in for a share of his humor. He told James of her frightened look the day she ran away from the " mansion," and how distressed she felt at the thought of being idle. James laughed heartily at this, and Annie blushed very red, but soon recovered sufficiently to detail, in a very arch way, too, the annoyances she had experienced from the Scotchman, and the ill-luck that cavalier met with at the hands of Larry Ryan.

This amused James beyond measure, and he requested Annie—just as if she were going to please him !—to show how she looked and frowned when the Scotchman offered her his snuff-box.

Thus time passed till midnight, when O'Rourke, who told Annie to be watching for him at an early hour in the morning, went down to his hotel, and the little party broke up.

If we were the most truthful historian in the world, we would not risk our reputation by asserting that James or Annie slept a wink till morning. The former was waiting, accompanied by the gentleman whom he had spoken to outside

the church, when Mr. Ryan opened the door, and
Annie was more than two—no, we will not tell it
on her now—Annie was already dressed, and
when Francis came, and all the others who had
been there the previous night, there was a neat
little wedding-party after all.

Little Annie! a man a thousand degrees less
noble than James O'Rourke might have gone
wild with joy at leading you off to be his bride.
You blush so much that your blue eyes sparkle
the more. You make so many mistakes, and you
are so forgetful this morning, that it is bewitch-
ing to see your little puzzled look. In short, go
on, Annie ; everything you do this morning makes
you look the prettier.

Miss Sweeny is a **very** handsome bridesmaid,
but is greatly afraid of the portly groomsman,
who thinks James O'Rourke one of the luckiest
men in America. The party went to the church
early in the day, and, the important ceremony
being performed, the happy bride and groom left
the city that evening for a short tour through the
States. When they returned, James purchased
a house in a beautiful part of New York City,
from which himself and Mrs. O'Rourke, and
quite a number of little O'Rourkes, may be seen
driving to the Central Park every Sunday evening.

And now we will turn from our happy hero and heroine, and take leave of those other valuable people who have borne us company through our story. John G. Ryan being the most illustrious, of course we must greet him first. He yet continues to thrive in his old path, and his bitterest enemy could not wish him worse; for there is an uplifted Hand sustained by Mercy, but which Justice one day compels to fall heavily on such as he.

Farrell Reilly and his wife have long since left the castle cottage, and are now living contentedly with Miles O'Rourke, in a neat little house with ivy-covered walls, within view of the beautiful bay of Queenstown.

Mr. Lacy teaches school yet, but has grown somewhat deaf, which renders him so cross that he is the terror of all the boys in the neighborhood. His evening walks are less frequent now, and always terminate at Nancy Brady's cabin. Nancy, who, to use her own words, "wants for nothing," is always very glad to see him, because their chat is all about their old neighbors whom both loved so well.

Miss Sweeny is now Mrs. Somebody, the mistress of a handsome rural homestead. Her father and mother still live in the little white and green dwelling, happy and contented.

www.ingramcontent.com/pod-product-compliance
Lightning Source LLC
Chambersburg PA
CBHW030807020726
47499CB00006B/1799